The Haunted Schoolhouse

THE HAUNTED SCHOOLHOUSE

an Adventure Club Book

By Johnathan Rand

Illustrations by Darrin Brege

An AudioCraft Publishing, Inc. book

This book is a work of fiction. Names, places, characters and incidents are used fictitiously, or are products of the author's very active imagination.

Warehouse security provided by Abby, Lily Munster, & Scooby-Boo

The Haunted Schoolhouse
ISBN 1-893699-73-0

Grateful acknowledgment is made for permission to reprint excerpts from the following copyrighted material:

"The Legend, '97" by Bob Farley. Copyright © 1997 Mindstage/WTCM Radio, Inc., Traverse City 49684
Used by permission

Printed in USA

First Printing - January 2006

TABLE OF CONTENTS

AUTHOR'S NOTE

The stories in the Adventure Club series have become some of my very favorite works. My life as a boy was not unlike the six kids that I write about. My days were filled with dreaming and doing, creating and crafting. It's my hope that, as you read these stories, perhaps you see a little of yourself in one of these characters.

I am often asked if 'Great Bear Heart' really exists, and the answer is—

Yes.

I have changed the name from its original 'Indian' name. Should you happen upon the small town of 'Great Bear Heart', located in northern lower Michigan, you'll find that most of the places I've written about—including the old haunted schoolhouse—really are there.

But most importantly, Great Bear Heart exists in your mind. It exists in the hearts of six kids who thirst for adventure and long for a excitement. For them, Great Bear Heart has always been there . . . and always will be.

My thanks to Lynn DeGrande for her editing work, and to Devan Beagle for his expert advance proofreading.

-Johnathan Rand
January 3, 2006

THE HAUNTED SCHOOLHOUSE

1

In October, the tiny town of Great Bear Heart undergoes a radical change. The northern Michigan summer has dwindled to a distant memory, and the nights are colder, warning of the coming winter. The air has a bite to it, a peculiar ice-cream texture that brushes your skin like a cool sheet. When you breathe it in, you can feel the chill right to the bottom of your lungs.

Even the smells are different. The scents of barbeques, of sticky pine and musky cedar, and the delicate aromas of wildflowers are gone, replaced with the occasional, pungent odor of burning leaves.

And the animals act differently, too. There's a

heightened urgency in the scamper of chipmunks and squirrels as they gather food for the winter. More birds appear at the feeders, wolfing down loads of seeds. The animals sense the coming winter, and they busily prepare for the long, cold months ahead.

But the most dramatic transformation comes in the way of colors. Gone are the lush, thick greens of summer. Maples, oaks, and other trees display brilliant leaves of red, orange, purple, crimson, yellow, bronze, copper, and gold. The entire countryside is engulfed in a display of colors that are only seen once a year. Even the clouds are different. In October, their giant bellies take on a steely-gray hue, and they sail slowly across an ocean of blue sky like magnificent iron ships, their mammoth hulls rimmed with fiery white.

After a few weeks, the colors fade. The leaves lose their vibrant shades, wither, turn brown, and fall from the trees. Those that remain are yanked and tugged by the harsh October winds until they, too, are sent flying across the sky, twisting and turning, fluttering and falling to the earth.

And for the six of us in the Adventure Club—Shane Mitchell, Tony Gritter, Lyle Haywood, Holly O'Mara, Dylan Bunker, and me, Parker Smith—October in Great Bear Heart meant just one thing:

Halloween.

But for us, the holiday meant much more than trick-or-treating. Halloween meant dressing up in fun costumes. It meant parties at school, pumpkin carving, and caramel-dipped apples. It meant a shiny, silver moon gazing down through clear, chilly nights, and bats flittering through an inky, star-studded sky. It meant reading scary stories out loud in our clubhouse high in a maple tree not far from Devil's Ridge.

However, Halloween never really *scared* us. I mean . . . we all read scary stories. We dressed up like ghosts or goblins or witches or mummies . . . but that's all it ever was. Pretend. We didn't *believe* in that sort of stuff . . . we were just having fun.

But this year, Halloween was going to mean something entirely different. This Halloween, we would have an experience that still freaks us out to this day. In fact, most of us in the club don't even talk about it anymore. Sure, we've had some scary things happen to us. We had a weird experience at Devil's Ridge when we were playing a prank on the Martin brothers, who happen to be the three biggest goofballs in Great Bear Heart. If there was trouble to be found, you can bet that the Martin brothers weren't far away. They didn't like us, and we didn't like them . . . which was just fine. Then, there was the really creepy day that we spent at Grand Hotel on Mackinac Island. Plus, we restored an old research submarine . . . only to have it spring a leak in Puckett Lake. We didn't think we were going to get out alive. And we had been caught in a forest fire . . . and let me tell you: *that* was *scary.*

But what happened *this* Halloween was going to be far freakier than anything else that had ever happened to us . . . and it all started at our weekly meeting high in a tree, in our clubhouse tucked away in the forest.

2

Our clubhouse is really cool. We built it in a maple tree in the middle of the woods, complete with separate, multi-level rooms and a lookout. In the summer, when the leaves are thick and full, it's nearly invisible. We built it with scrap wood from Mr. Beansworth's old barn, which wasn't too far away. The barn had collapsed, and Mr. Beansworth let us have the wood for free.

Five of us were there, waiting for Dylan Bunker, who was always fifteen minutes late for our meetings. Holly O'Mara was seated near an open window, gently stroking

cat, who was sleeping on her
that we'd found in an old shed
ome a loyal pal and our official
as amazing: he'd climb the tree
lubhouse, and then climb all the
e left. Lyle joked that the cat was

Tony Gritter was shooting a rubber band at a knot in one of the boards on the ceiling, catching the band when it fell, aiming, and shooting once again. Lyle Haywood was talking quietly with Shane Mitchell, our club president, about ways that we could earn some money during the fall and winter months. Earning money always seemed to be a prime focus for us, since most of the fun things that we wanted to do always cost money. Holly, our club treasurer, had reported at our last meeting that we had less than thirty dollars in our club savings, and Shane had given us the order to start thinking about ways we could earn money. Now we were gathered high in our clubhouse, waiting for Dylan Bunker, so we could discuss our ideas.

Tony made a wild shot with his rubber band. It bounced off the ceiling, struck the wall, and tumbled out the open window. He frowned and looked at his watch.

"Geez . . . where *is* that guy?" he asked. "He's always

late."

"It hasn't been fifteen minutes yet," I said, looking at my own watch. "My guess is that he'll be getting here right about . . . *now.*"

Suddenly, the rope ladder that extended down from the trap door in the floor began to shake. We heard a grunt and a groan from below, and several gasps. Then Dylan's mop of red hair popped up through the opening in the floor.

"Hey, guys!" he chirped, out of breath from the twenty-foot climb. He reached out and clumsily pulled himself into the clubhouse. "Sorry I'm late."

"What's new?" Tony snapped. "You're *always* late."

Dylan shrugged, as if the very thought that someone could be offended by his tardiness was some new and strange idea.

"All right, let's get the meeting started," Shane said. "Lyle has some cool ideas about things we can do to earn some money."

Lyle nodded and pulled out a pad of paper. "Okay," he began as he adjusted his glasses. "There's a lot of things we can do. For starters, we could sell candy bars, like we did at school. If we—"

Lyle stopped speaking when he saw Holly shaking her head. Dollar opened his eyes, shifted in Holly's lap, and went back to sleep.

"We already talked about that, remember?" Holly said. "It'll cost too much to buy the candy bars. We'd have to raise the price to make money, and people aren't going to pay more than what they would at the store."

Lyle shrugged, then made several pencil scratches in his notebook. "Okay," he said. "How about an apple cider stand? We could have it down at the park, like we did when we sold food and drinks to the people who came to town to look for Bigfoot."

I smiled. One time we played a prank on Norm Beeblemeyer, the local newspaper reporter for the *Great Bear Heart Times*. Shane made two giant feet out of wood, and Tony strapped them to his shoes and made 'Bigfoot' tracks all around town. The joke got way out of hand, and people came from all over to hunt for Bigfoot. We earned oodles of money selling hot dogs, hamburgers, and juice at a roadside stand that we set up across from the Great Bear Heart Market.

"But that was different," I said. "That was summertime, and a lot of people were in town. This is October. All of the tourists and summer residents have gone home. I don't think business would be very good."

"I saw a thing on television about some kids who put together their own carnival in somebody's back yard,"

Tony said. "They had games and contests, and they charged money for people to enter."

"That would be fun," Holly said. "But what if it rains? Then we would have to hold the carnival indoors, and there isn't any place in Great Bear Heart that would be big enough."

Holly was right about that. Great Bear Heart is a tiny town in northern lower Michigan, on the shores of Puckett Lake. It was named after Potowatami Indian Chief Great Bear Heart, way back in the 1800s. Our town has a post office, a library, an historical museum, a market, a hardware store, a township hall, a fire station, a bar and grill called *Rollers*, a strip of rental cottages called *Lazy Shores Resort,* and a small restaurant called *The Kona.* There's also a really cool park and beach area right behind the library, across from the market. We go swimming there in the summer.

But there really isn't a place big enough to set up an indoor carnival.

About this time, I noticed that Shane, our club president, hadn't said anything for a few minutes. Shane is usually pretty talkative . . . unless he has an idea. Then he just kind of stares up into space—until he starts grinning. When he starts grinning, he's got an idea. Usually, when Shane Mitchell gets an idea, you can bet ten times out of ten that it's a *good* one.

And right now, Shane's grin was so wide that you could see every single one of his upper row of teeth.

After a moment, we all stopped speaking and just looked at him. He looked at us, and his grin never faded. "Guys," he said, scratching his chin, "it's time once again for the Adventure Club to get into the haunting business."

None of us said a word as he began to explain his idea.

3

"A haunted house!" Shane exclaimed, glancing around. I was a little puzzled, and I think the rest of us were, too.

"You know what I mean, guys!" Shane said. "We find a place and put together a haunted house! Then we charge a dollar admission for people to go through it, like they did at that school last year!"

"Oh, yeah," Dylan said. "I remember that. That was cool."

"Yeah," Tony agreed. "That *was* fun!"

Shane continued. "Remember how they decorated some of the rooms? They had a coffin that opened up, and there was a mummy inside?"

"That was *scary,*" Holly said.

"Yeah," I said. "When that coffin lid opened and that thing popped out, I about jumped out of my skin!"

"That's what I'm talking about!" Shane said. "The school did it as a fund-raiser! We could do the same thing! We could set up a haunted house and charge people admission to walk through it! We could do it Halloween weekend, which would mean we wouldn't get to go trick-or-treating."

I shrugged. "So what?" I said. "I'd rather earn money! A haunted house would be great!"

"It would be *awesome!"* Tony trumpeted. "We could scare people . . . and get paid to do it!"

"We could make a ghost on a wire, like we did at Devil's Ridge!" Dylan chimed in.

Lyle Haywood raised his hands in caution. "Guys, guys," he said, "a haunted house might be a lot of fun . . . and we might be able to make some money doing it. But where are we going to have it? It's just like Tony's carnival idea . . . there isn't a place in Great Bear Heart big enough for something like that."

Once again, reality set in. A haunted house would be a lot of fun . . . but where would we host it?

"Maybe we could do it outside," Tony suggested. "You know . . . like some kind of haunted trail through the woods, where people could walk through at night."

"Yeah," I replied, "but like Holly said: what if it rains? If the weather is cold and rainy, nobody will want to walk through the woods. Especially at night."

"Wait a minute," Holly said. "Why don't we do it at the township hall? I mean . . . it's not big enough for a carnival, but we could probably turn it into a haunted house for a few days."

The Great Bear Heart township hall is located right between the hardware store and the Great Bear Heart Market. There is a large hall, a kitchen area, and several offices. Also, located in the same building, is the fire department. It's an all-volunteer department, so no one is there . . . unless, of course, there's a fire somewhere.

"That place would be *perfect,*" Lyle said. "The only question is . . . would we be allowed to use it?"

"It belongs to the township," Shane said, "so it belongs to everyone who lives here. I know some people have wedding receptions and banquets and things like that at the hall. All we'd have to do is go to a township meeting and ask for permission."

"The next meeting is tomorrow night at seven, at the township hall," Holly said. "I know, because my dad goes to all the meetings."

"Let's take a vote, then," Shane said. "All in favor of making a haunted house to earn some money, raise your hand."

All six of us raised our hands.

"Who can make it to the township meeting tomorrow night?" he asked.

Again, we raised our hands.

"Okay," he continued. "The matter is settled. Let's meet at the market at ten minutes to seven, tomorrow night."

That closed the meeting, and we took turns descending the rope ladder that dangled from our clubhouse. Dollar scrambled down the tree like an Olympic raccoon. When we were all on the ground, Lyle pulled out a remote control from his pocket. He and Shane had set up the rope ladder with the remote, so a button could be pressed to retract it, raising it up to the clubhouse. That way, if anyone happened upon our fort, they wouldn't be able to get to it very easily. And of course, the same remote control was used to lower the rope. It was pretty nifty.

We hiked through the woods, following the trail that snaked back to Great Bear Heart Mail Route Road and into town. From there, we went separate ways . . . except for Holly and me. She lives near my house, so we walked home together.

"Do you think they'll let us use the township hall to

make our haunted house?" I asked.

"I don't know," she said. "But I don't see why not."

We were pretty hopeful—and pretty certain—that the township board would allow us to go ahead with our plans for a haunted house.

Boy, were we in for a big surprise.

4

The six of us sat on metal folding chairs in the small township hall board room. There were about a dozen adults seated, as well. I recognized a couple of them, along with Holly's father. At the front of the room, seated at a desk and facing us, were the five township board members. When they asked if anyone had any new business to discuss, Shane raised his hand. He explained what we wanted to do and why.

The board members looked at one another and shrugged, but the supervisor shook his head. "I don't think that we can allow you to use the hall right now," he said.

We were stunned. We had been certain that we'd be able to use the hall.

"But why not?" Lyle asked. "We won't be doing any damage to it."

"Yeah, we're not going to hurt anything," Tony piped. "We just want to make a haunted house."

Again, the supervisor shook his head. "Guys, I think it's a great idea, and it probably would be a lot of fun. And I think it's great that you want to do something to earn money. But the problem is, there's going to be some renovation work going on, beginning next week. New carpeting, and some repairs to the roof. There'll be too much going on for anyone to be using the township hall. Now, if you want to wait until November when the remodeling is done, we could probably arrange something."

November? I thought. *Who ever heard of a haunted house in November? October is the month for haunted houses.*

We nodded. We were disappointed, but we understood.

"Well, we really wanted to have our haunted house in October, with Halloween coming up," Shane said.

"Sorry guys," the supervisor replied. "I wish we

could help you out. Maybe next year."

The next order of business was taken up. Holly's dad was mad about some lady in town that was using a leaf blower all hours of the day and night. He said it was really loud, and that she was doing it just to annoy the neighbors. We listened for a while, but it was really boring. Shane finally caught our attention, hiked his thumb toward the door, and nodded. We excused ourselves and left the meeting.

"Should've figured," Tony said, as we stepped outside into the chilly night. "Another great idea, shot down in flames."

"It sure would've been fun," Dylan said.

The evening was gloomy and dark. A thin veil of fog hung like a smoky curtain, giving the streetlights a wide, round aura. The sun had set an hour ago, but the lights from the nearby market lit up the entire village. Of course, there isn't a lot to light up in Great Bear Heart. Across the street from the market sat the Great Bear Heart Library and the historical museum, which were visible in the soupy light. Behind the library and the museum was Puckett Park, set on the banks of Puckett Lake. A cool wind blew across the water, and we could hear the unseen waves lapping the shoreline.

"Let's go get some hot chocolate at the market,"

Holly suggested. That sounded good, so we started out.

Several cars were parked outside. A woman was pumping gas, and a man was putting air into his tires. We strode inside, squinting beneath the bright white lights.

"Hey, guys," Mr. Bloomer said from behind the counter. George Bloomer owns the market, and we all like him. He helped us out a lot when we had our roadside stand and sold food and drinks.

"Hi," we replied in unison.

He must have sensed our gloominess, because he frowned from behind the counter. "What's wrong?" he said.

"We wanted to use the township hall to have a haunted house this Halloween," I explained. "We thought that we could charge an admission fee and make a little extra money."

"But the township board won't let us," Shane said.

"Why not?" Mr. Bloomer asked.

"They're doing some remodeling," Holly said with a shrug. "They said that we wouldn't be able to use it until November."

"Well, that's a bummer," Mr. Bloomer said.

"For sure," Dylan said. "We could've had a lot of fun."

"Do you know of a place we could use to make a

haunted house?" I asked.

Mr. Bloomer stroked his chin. "Not right off the top of my head," he said. "But if I think of anything, I'll let you know."

We bought six hot chocolates and sipped them outside. In the chill of the October night, the warm, sweet liquid tasted good.

"Okay," Shane said. "Let's think of something else. It's not the end of the world."

While Shane was right, we were still disappointed. Making a haunted house would have been fun . . . on top of the fact that we could have earned some money.

So we gave up thinking about making a haunted house, and tried to come up with other ideas. We left that night with a homework assignment: each one of us was to write a list of ten moneymaking ideas and bring them to school the following day. We would discuss the ideas during lunch hour.

I worked really hard, and came up with some pretty good ideas before I went to bed.

But it was Shane Mitchell who came up with the wildest idea of all. At school the next day, he didn't have a list of ten moneymaking ideas. At lunchtime, he ordered an emergency meeting of the Adventure Club at six o'clock that evening, and said that our plans to make a haunted house were still on. He needed a couple of hours, he said, to make sure his idea would work.

Later that evening in our clubhouse, Shane explained what he had in mind . . . and I'll tell you right now, when he told us where he wanted to make our haunted house, the five of us—Holly, Lyle, Dylan, Tony, and me—weren't excited.

We were *terrified.*

5

"The old schoolhouse on Oak Street!" Shane said, his face glowing. "It would be the best place of all!"

We were sitting on milk crates in our clubhouse. The evening was crisp and cool, and we were all wearing sweatshirts except for Dylan, who was wearing his winter coat. A couple of candles were lit, because the sun was setting sooner and it got dark earlier.

After Shane spoke, no one said a word. Dylan gasped a little. Holly raised her eyes and looked at me.

Outside, a cold wind slipped through the trees.

Branches trembled. Leaves, dry and brittle, cracked like old bones in the breeze. Dollar was curled up in Holly's lap, sleeping.

Finally, Lyle spoke.

"But Shane," he said quietly, "the old schoolhouse on Oak Street is *already* haunted. That's why it's boarded up."

"The ghost of Reginald Perrywinkle lives there," Dylan said with a shudder.

"Oh, come on!" Shane said. "That's just an old wives' tale! There's no ghost of anybody at the old schoolhouse!" He looked around at each of us. "It's not haunted . . . unless we want it to be."

There was a long, eerie silence. The old, red brick schoolhouse at the corner of Great Bear Heart Mail Route Road and Oak Street has been boarded up since before we were even born. There's a playground behind it that some kids still use, along with a big, fenced-in field where we play softball. Several towering oak and maple trees grow close, their limbs intertwining and knitted together, shading the schoolhouse from the sun during the summer months. Dad said that he went to school there as a kid, but as the town grew, so did the need for a bigger school. Nowadays, all of us in Great Bear Heart ride a bus and go to school in Indian River.

But there are stories about the old schoolhouse. A long, long time ago, there was a headmaster named Reginald Perrywinkle, who was not a very nice man. He told all of the students that, after he died, his ghost was going to come back from his grave and haunt the old schoolhouse.

Well, not long after he died, odd things started happening at the school. Mostly little things, like strange noises from the basement. At night, people claimed they saw a lantern in what once had been Reginald Perrywinkle's office. One morning, students arrived at school to find all of the books in the school library taken from the shelves and stacked neatly on the floor. The building had been locked all night; no one could figure out how the books had been moved.

Stories began to circulate around town. Some people believed that old Reginald Perrywinkle had made good on his threat, after all. They believed he really *had* returned from the grave . . . and his ghost was haunting the old schoolhouse. My dad told me about some of the things that happened while he was in school, but he didn't believe the stories about the ghost of Reginald Perrywinkle. He said that people had a way of letting their imaginations get the best of them.

Shane could tell that we weren't very thrilled with his

idea, and he spoke again.

"Look, guys," he urged. "Those stories about that old fuddy-duddy haunting the school are just that: *stories.* People just made them up."

"How do *you* know?" Tony asked.

Shane folded his arms. "I guess I don't know for sure. But think about it: wouldn't the old schoolhouse be a great place for our haunted house? We could decorate different rooms and scare people as they walked through. We could even build a coffin and have a mummy inside it, like we saw last year at the school. I'll bet people would come from all over the county!"

"That would be cool," Holly said warily, but I could tell she was a little nervous about Shane's idea.

"Okay," Lyle Haywood began, "let's just say we decide to do it. How do we get permission?"

"I've already got it," Shane replied proudly. "Last night, I got a call from Mr. Bloomer at the market. He said he'd been thinking about our haunted house idea, and suggested we use the old schoolhouse. It belongs to the township, just like the town hall . . . so after school today, I went over to the supervisor's house. He thought the old schoolhouse would be a great place for our haunted house, and said we could use it if we want."

"I'm not making a haunted house in a haunted

house," Dylan said defiantly. He shuddered. "I don't even like going *near* that place."

Holly spoke. "But what if it *is* haunted, Shane?"

"We won't know unless we try," Shane answered. "Let's go inside and check it out ourselves. Look what I've got." He dug into his pocket, then held out his fist. When he opened his hand, he was holding an old skeleton key.

"Where'd you get that?!?!" I gasped.

"The township supervisor gave it to me," he replied. "It's a master key. He said it opens both doors—the front and the back—plus all of the doors inside."

"Does . . . does it work?" Tony stammered.

"There's one way to find out," Shane replied, flipping the skeleton key up into the air and catching it as it descended. "Anybody wanna go check it out?"

Wind shook the tree, causing our clubhouse to sway gently. The candles flickered, but they didn't go out. Dollar stirred in Holly's lap.

"Tonight?" Holly asked quietly.

"Sure," Shane said, pulling a small flashlight from his back pocket. "I came prepared."

Tony raised his hand hesitantly and glanced around. "I'll go if everyone else does," he said.

I raised my hand. Lyle raised his, followed by Holly.

"Actually, it might be kind of fun," Holly said, "if we all go together."

"Geez, I don't know, guys," Dylan whimpered. "My dad wants me to, uh, um . . . he wants me to . . . to rake the leaves in our yard. Yeah."

"At night?!?!" Tony needled. "Don't be silly! You're just afraid to go into the old schoolhouse."

"But it's dark," Dylan protested.

"Shane has a flashlight," Holly said to Dylan. "Besides . . . we'll all be together."

Dylan heaved a sigh, then shrugged and sighed heavily. "Okay," he said, raising his hands in defeat. "But let's not stay too long."

The matter was settled. For the first time in years, the old schoolhouse would be unlocked. And for the first time in as many years, students would once again set foot in the shadowy hallways.

Six students, exactly.

Click. Ker-chunk.

The old lock protested loudly as Shane turned the key. Then, he tried the doorknob, but it didn't work.

"Try turning the key in the other direction," Lyle said. "Sometimes old locks work the opposite way."

Shane turned the key counterclockwise. There were some more clicks and clunks, and Shane tried the knob again.

It turned.

"Bingo," Shane said. He pulled the door open, and

the hinges groaned like a giant, lazy monster. Stale air washed over us, and Shane pointed the light inside.

The hallway was murky, and a layer of chalky dust glazed the wood floor. It was like gazing into an abandoned mine shaft.

The six of us just stood there, staring into the gloom. Now that we were actually *here,* facing the ancient brick beast that had been asleep for so long, we weren't sure if we actually wanted to go inside. Even Shane seemed apprehensive, but it was he who broke our spell and led the way.

"School's in session, guys," he said quietly, and he stepped through the door. He swung the flashlight beam down the hall. Shadows scattered and leapt. We followed in a group, a tight little knot of kids glancing warily about, bound together like a blob of denim and sweatshirts. Holly carried Dollar in her arms. It was difficult to see with just one flashlight, but I could make out darkened doorways on either side of us. There was a closed door at the end of the hall.

"This place is creepy," Dylan peeped.

"The creepier the better," Shane said. "After all . . . if we're making a haunted house to scare people, what better place than somewhere that's already spooky-looking?"

He sure was right about that. As we walked slowly down the hallway, our feet whispering on the dusty floor, I couldn't help but think about ghosts and spooks and things that go bump in the night. The walls seemed to close in on us, like the entire schoolhouse was a living, breathing thing, a single animal, a hundred years old, glaring back at us through the darkness.

But maybe *that* was it. It was night time, and it was very dark. Maybe the old schoolhouse wouldn't seem so creepy and menacing during the day.

We came to an open door, and Shane swept the beam inside. It was a classroom, completely empty. The windows on the far wall were boarded up. There were no desks, no tables or chairs. The only thing left behind was a long chalkboard on the wall at the front of the room.

On the other side of the hall was another classroom that looked identical to the one we'd just checked out.

"Looks like everybody's cutting class," Tony snickered.

We continued down the hall. To the right, a hallway opened up, leading to another classroom. In front of us was an engraved sign mounted on the closed door.

Holly read the sign out loud. *"Headmaster,"* she breathed, her voice just above a whisper.

A chill went through my body as I remembered the

stories about Reginald Perrywinkle's ghost returning to haunt the schoolhouse to scare all of the students. Even if his ghost *hadn't* returned, the stories of the old headmaster had succeeded in scaring *me.*

Silently, Shane dug the skeleton key from his sweatshirt pocket.

"Maybe we should wait until tomorrow," Dylan said.

"Stop being a pansy," Tony retorted.

"I'm not being a pansy!" Dylan protested.

"You are, too."

"Am not!"

"It's probably empty, just like all the other rooms," Shane said, ignoring Tony and Dylan's bickering. He slipped the ancient key into the lock, and gave it a twist. Then he grasped the knob.

Now, Shane is usually right about most things. Not always, of course.

And this was one of those times.

The old headmaster's office *wasn't* empty.

We just didn't know it . . . until Shane pulled the knob, and opened the door.

7

As soon as Shane opened the door, the flashlight beam illuminated much more than an empty room.

In the middle of the office was a large desk. A chair sat behind it. Both were covered with a fine layer of dust. The desk displayed several items: an old book, some pencils, and a ruler, all glazed with dust.

"Wow," Lyle whispered. *"They left the headmaster's stuff here."*

"I doubt it's Perrywinkle's," Shane said. "He wasn't the last headmaster here at the school."

"I wonder why they left everything," Holly mused. "There are even pictures on the walls."

And there were, too. Shane directed the beam of light upward, where several pictures hung from the walls. One of them contained old black-and-white portraits of nearly a dozen people.

"What's that one?" Tony asked, pointing.

Shane stepped into the dark office, training the light directly on the picture.

"It looks like these are the guys who were headmasters of the school," Shane replied. "There are names written beneath each portrait." He started reading slowly, as if he were having a difficult time making out the names. "Frederick Jacobsen . . . Gordon Wil . . . Wilshire . . . Richard Peabody . . . ."

And suddenly—

"Oh my gosh!" Shane gasped. *"There he is!"*

Shane nearly shouted the words, causing all of us to jump.

"Reginald Perrywinkle!" Shane continued. *"There's a picture of him, right there!"*

We drew closer, crowding around to see.

"Wow," Tony said. The rest of us were silent, gazing at the picture.

A term popped into my head . . . something that

Shane said earlier in the clubhouse.

Fuddy-duddy.

That's what Reginald Perrywinkle looked like. An old fuddy-duddy. He had a thick, white beard and a bushy, caterpillar-like mustache that draped over his lips. His white hair was short and slicked back, and his eyes were cold and unpleasant. His face held a scornful scowl, and I wondered if he was angry with the whole world.

"He doesn't look like a very nice guy," Holly said.

"He looks mean," Dylan said.

I looked at some of the other portraits. The other men weren't smiling, either, but they looked confident and proud. I looked again at the picture of Reginald Perrywinkle, and I could easily imagine him trying to scare the students. I sure wouldn't want him to be *my* headmaster.

"Let's keep going," Shane said. "We still have to check out the bell tower and the basement."

We shuffled out of the office, and Shane closed and locked the door. Gradually, my fears eased. As we walked slowly down the hallway, I realized that my dad was right. The stories of old Reginald Perrywinkle were just made up by superstitious people. It made interesting gossip around town, but the fact was that the ghost of Reginald Perrywinkle didn't haunt the old schoolhouse.

But *we* would. We were going to haunt it, and in a big way. We were going to make the best haunted house ever, and we'd earn a lot of money when people came to walk through it.

"This way," Shane said, walking down the hallway. "The bell tower should be over here somewhere."

We walked in a tight, huddled group, moving slowly, following the flashlight beam as Shane swept it about. The wood floor creaked beneath our feet. Then the hallway ended at the back door of the building.

"That's odd," Shane said, tracking the flashlight beam above his head. "The bell should be right above us. There's nothing here but the ceiling."

Suddenly, a shrill, booming *bong!* exploded from above like thunder. Holly let out a shriek, and Dollar leapt from her arms, landing on the floor. Dylan screamed. My body turned to ice.

The bell of the old schoolhouse was ringing . . . all by itself!

8

One, two, three times.

Bong! Bong! Bong!

"Let's get out of here!" Dylan squealed. *"I'm freaked out! I'm totally freaked out!"*

Suddenly, Tony started laughing. Shane spun and shined the flashlight in his face. In the glow, we could clearly see what Tony had done.

Near the wall was an old rope that dangled through a small hole in the ceiling. In the darkness, we hadn't seen it.

"That was hilarious!" Tony said, and he grabbed the rope and rang the bell again. "I felt the rope brush my arm, and I figured that it was for the bell. I gave 'er a good yank. You guys just about passed out!"

"Yeah, real funny," Lyle scolded. "You doofus!"

"Hey, you would have done the same thing," Tony replied. "Come on . . . don't be so uptight. It was just a joke."

My heart was still jack-hammering in my chest. The loud *bong!* sure had surprised me. When you get scared like that, it takes a while to calm down.

"Let's check out the basement," Shane said. "Maybe the ghost of Reginald Perrywinkle is down there."

"He is not!" Dylan said.

"Take it easy," Shane replied. "I'm only kidding. We've been walking around in here for five minutes. Anybody see a ghost?"

"No, but there's a clown standing right next to me," Holly said, and she nudged Tony with her elbow. He grunted and snickered.

Holly picked up Dollar and we walked back down the hallway, following our footprints in the layer of dust until we came to the basement door. Once again, Shane pulled out the skeleton key and inserted it into the lock. The key turned easily, and Shane grasped the knob and pulled.

The door opened with the loudest, deepest creak I have ever heard. It rumbled and rolled like a bowling ball down an alley, echoing through the schoolhouse and the basement.

"Geez, somebody needs to oil the hinges," Lyle said.

"No," I said. "Let's leave the doors the way they are. The creaking sounds scary. That's just what we want when we make our haunted house."

"Right on, Parker," Shane said. "We want our customers scared out of their wits!"

He shined the light down the cement steps. There was even more dust on the stairs than there was in the hallway. That would be something we would have to clean up. If the dust was stirred up, our customers would be sneezing their heads off.

"Last one down is a rotten egg," Shane said, taking the first step. None of us, however, were in that big of a hurry. We all stayed close together as we made our way to the belly of the old schoolhouse.

When we reached the last few steps, we stopped. The air was different down here: colder, muskier. It felt thick and heavy, like breathing through a cool blanket.

The basement floor was made of bricks. Like the stairs, it was covered with a thick layer of dust. Shane shined the light around, but there wasn't anything to see. The basement was empty.

"Perfect!" Shane exclaimed. "There's nothing here. I was afraid we'd have to haul out a bunch of junk."

"When do we start?" Tony asked.

"Well, first things first," Shane said. "Can everybody make it if we have a meeting tomorrow right after school? We can meet right here at the schoolhouse again."

We all agreed.

"Good," Shane continued. "We can go through this place again in the daylight. We'll need to start thinking about things we can rig up for scary effects."

"Let's build a coffin!" Dylan exclaimed. "Just like they did at the school! When people walk by, the coffin lid will open, and a mummy will pop out!"

"We might do that," Shane said. "But we need to put our heads together. Let's go."

We turned around and headed up the steps. Shane closed and locked the basement door. Then we walked out the front door. Shane inserted the key in the lock, and gave it a turn. Then he gave the knob a shake to make sure the door was secure.

"Okay," he said, "tomorrow after school. Let's meet right here on the steps."

We said our good-byes, then we disbanded and went home. Holly and I walked together until we reached my house. I told her goodnight, and went inside.

And the more I thought about our haunted house project, the more excited I became. Shane was right: the old schoolhouse *was* perfect. It was spooky, creepy, eerie, and strange . . . all rolled into one.

I was proud of myself, too. Up until tonight, I had been spooked by the old building. Tonight, five of my friends and I had gone *inside* the old schoolhouse on Oak Street. We weren't scared—except when Tony rang the bell—and we hadn't seen any ghosts.

But the following afternoon, something happened.

Something none of us could explain.

And now, as I look back on the events that took place at the old schoolhouse, we should have known that there was more to the ghost stories than we realized.

We should have realized that when Reginald Perrywinkle told his students that he was going to come back from the grave to haunt the school, he wasn't kidding around . . . he was *serious.*

9

The next day was cold and windy. Brown leaves whirled through the air like swarms of sparrows, and the sky was gray and gloomy. The trees, which had been so colorful and beautiful only a few weeks ago, now showed much of their bony, knotted limbs. In a few weeks the branches would be completely bare, and they would reach for the sky like thin, gnarled fingers.

We all wore our winter coats that day, and Holly wore her knit hat and gloves. She had brought Dollar with her, cradling the cat in her arms and stroking his head. Although Dollar was our official club mascot, Holly took care of him, keeping him at her house. A portion of our club membership dues paid for his food and kitty litter.

We waited on the steps for Dylan Bunker, who was, of course, his usual fifteen minutes late. Soon, we saw him huffing and puffing, running up the hill toward us. He also had on his winter coat, along with his snowmobile boots, thick gloves, and a blue knit hat with a yellow dingle-ball on the top. His hat was pulled down too far over his eyebrows, and he had to cock his head back just to see straight.

"Man," he said, as he reached the cement steps that rose to the front door of the old schoolhouse. "I hope it doesn't stay this cold when we have our haunted house!"

"It's supposed to get warmer in a day or two," Lyle said. "Actually, it's supposed to get back up to seventy degrees by the end of the week."

"I hope so," Tony said with a shudder. "This weather is for the birds."

"Just be glad it's not snowing," Shane said with a grimace.

"Hey, I don't mind the snow," Tony said, his teeth chattering. "It's just that summer doesn't last long enough. And winter is too long."

"I'll be sure to tell the weatherman that," I said with a grin. "Maybe he'll change some things around for you."

Shane dug into his pocket and pulled out the old skeleton key. "Okay," he began, "while it's still light out, let's walk through the school again. Holly, since you can draw the best, pay careful attention to everything, so you can make a sketch of what it looks like. We'll need it when we design the layout of our haunted house."

Holly nodded, and Shane continued. "The rest of us: let's get our imaginations going. Start thinking about things we can rig up to surprise people and give them a scare."

"Let's make a coffin with a mummy!" Dylan exclaimed. Of course, this wasn't the first time he'd brought up the mummy/coffin project. I think he mentioned it again just to make sure the rest of us wouldn't forget about it.

Shane slipped the old skeleton key into the lock, turned it, grasped the knob, and pulled. The door groaned open.

Even in the daylight, the hallway was murky and dark. Not as dark as last night, of course, but not much light came through the boarded-up windows.

"Why don't we take the boards off the windows?"

Dylan said. "Then we could see better."

"No," Shane said. "We want it to be dark."

"Yeah," Tony agreed. "Whoever heard of a haunted house that was bright on the inside?"

Shane took a step inside, and we followed. "Let's start with—"

He stopped speaking and walking at the same time. I was right behind him, and I bumped into his shoulder.

There was a long silence. We all saw what Shane was looking at, and we knew why he hadn't finished his sentence. It felt like the air had been sucked out of the school. It seemed hard to breathe. My skin crawled, like I was covered with hundreds of tiny spiders.

At the end of the hallway was the headmaster's office. Last night, Shane had closed and locked the door after we'd looked inside.

Now, the headmaster's door was wide open at the end of the dark hallway.

10

Nobody said a word for a long time. We just stared down the hallway at the open door.

Finally, Lyle spoke.

"Shane . . . did . . . did I just *imagine* that you closed and locked that door yesterday?"

"If you imagined it," Tony said, "then we all did. Shane closed and locked the door with the key."

"But how did it get open?" Holly said, shifting Dollar around in her arms. The cat had been sleeping, and awoke only briefly when he was moved. Then he went back to sleep.

"Has anyone been here besides us?" I asked.

Shane shook his head. "The township supervisor told me to be careful with the key because it was the only one he had," he said, holding up the skeleton key for all of us to see. "If this is the only key, then no one else is able to open any doors except us."

Slowly, we walked down the hallway toward the open door. When we passed the classrooms on the left and the right, I glanced nervously from side to side, wary of what I might see in the darkened rooms. Thankfully, they were empty . . . just like they had been yesterday.

But as we approached the end of the hallway, our eyes remained focused on the headmaster's door.

Someone . . . or some*thing* . . . had opened the door.

Who?

How?

Why?

"I'll bet it's the ghost of Reginald Perrywinkle," Dylan whispered.

"No, it's not," Shane said. "There's a perfectly logical explanation."

"Yeah," Tony said. "I'll bet little elves did it."

Holly snickered, and so did I. Sometimes Tony could be a bit sarcastic, but he could be pretty funny, too.

We stopped walking when we were only a few feet from the door. Shane reached out slowly and grasped the knob. He tried to turn it, but the knob wouldn't budge.

"Still locked," he said.

"But how can that be?" I asked. "If the door is open, it had to be unlocked somehow."

Shane closed the door slowly, and it fit snugly in the doorjamb. Without attempting to unlock it, he pulled it, and it opened.

"The lock is broken," Shane said. "It probably broke when I locked it yesterday. After all . . . it's pretty old."

"But how did it get open?" Holly asked. "Even if the lock was broken, you closed the door. It didn't open by itself."

"It might have," Lyle said, adjusting his glasses and inspecting the molding around the door. "All of this wood is warped. The door hasn't been open in years, until we opened it last night. It got really cold overnight, and that can cause the wood to shift. It was probably enough to pop the door open by itself."

"I still think that little elves did it," Tony said.

"Lyle's right," Shane said confidently. "It's nothing to worry about."

But we *did* have something to worry about.

Behind us, we heard a loud groan.

Door hinges.

Before we could even turn around, the front door of the schoolhouse slammed closed . . . leaving us in total darkness!

11

Panic and chaos exploded like wildfire. It was so dark that we couldn't see the floor, the walls, or the ceiling. We couldn't even see each other. Holly screamed, and so did Lyle. I yelled, too.

But when we all tried to run at the same time, it was like six frightened chickens in a barrel. We ran into each other, knocking and flailing about. Somebody fell, but it was too dark to see who went down. When I tried to move sideways, I tripped over whoever was on the floor, and fell down myself. I landed hard on my shoulder and winced in pain.

"Hey!" Shane shouted. "Everybody knock it off! Don't move! We're going to break our necks!"

We settled down.

"Somebody kicked me," Dylan said. He was the one who had fallen. I had tripped over him.

"That was me," I said, slowly getting to my feet. "I didn't mean to."

"Everybody settle down," Shane repeated. "We'll have to feel our way to the front door."

"Where's your flashlight?" Holly asked.

"I forgot it," Shane replied. "Come on."

Now that we weren't tripping all over each other, we carefully shuffled down the hallway, finding our way by feeling the wall with our hands.

"We're here," Shane said, and I heard the brass doorknob jiggle. I shuddered, because I was sure that the door wasn't going to open. I was sure that were locked in, and we'd never get out. Maybe the old schoolhouse really *was* haunted by the ghost of Reginald Perrywinkle, and he had trapped us inside.

But the door *did* open in a burst of gray light, and I don't think I've ever felt so relieved in my life.

All six of us tried to get out the door at the same time, and we got stuck. If anyone were watching, it

probably looked pretty funny: six scared kids, struggling and pushing, trying to get out the front door of the old schoolhouse.

Finally, we squeezed our way out, bounded down the steps, and stopped. We looked back at the old schoolhouse. Around and above us, the maples and oaks hissed in a heavy gust of wind. Leaves scrabbled at our feet.

Holly set Dollar on the ground, and the cat batted a few leaves before wandering over to inspect the trunk of a huge maple tree. "It must have been the wind," Holly said with relief. "That's all it was."

But she was wrong.

We heard snickering coming from the side of the building, then strained laughter, followed by a few snorts.

And there was no doubt who was making them. I'd recognize their whiny voices anywhere.

The Martin brothers. Gary, Larry, and Terry.

Then I saw movement. Larry's head, just for an instant, poked around the side of the schoolhouse.

Tony Gritter stormed toward them, and the five of us charged after him.

Sure enough, hiding on the side of the school were the three goofballs themselves, laughing and pointing at us.

"Gotcha!" Larry howled. "When we slammed the door closed, you guys freaked! We could hear you all the way out here!"

"And the whole town is going to hear *you* guys," Tony growled, doubling up his fists. He was ready to charge, but Shane and Lyle grabbed him by the shoulders and held him back.

"Leave 'em alone, Tony," Shane said. "They aren't worth it."

"You guys are nothing but chickens!" Terry taunted. "When we slammed that door closed, you guys blew a gasket!"

Holly shook her head and muttered something beneath her breath.

"What are you doing in this old place, anyway?" Larry asked snidely.

"None of your business," Tony snapped.

"You broke in, that's what you did," Gary said. "I'm going to call the cops."

"Go ahead," Shane replied with a careless shrug. "We have special permission to be in the schoolhouse."

"Yeah, right," Gary sneered.

"We do, too!" Dylan said defiantly. "We're going to make a haunt—"

Lyle suddenly reached up and cupped his hand over

Dylan's mouth, silencing him. *"They don't need to know what we're up to,"* he whispered. *"They'll just try and mess things up."*

Sooner or later, of course, the Martin's would figure out what we were doing. They might even try to mess with our plans . . . but for now, the less they knew, the better.

"Let's get out of here, guys," Larry said. "It's starting to smell."

The three Martins spun and trotted off, laughing and bumping each other.

"They'll never change," Holly said. Dollar had scampered to Holly's feet, and she scooped him up in her arms.

"Forget about them," Shane said. "We have more important things to think about. It's October tenth. We have nineteen days before we have to have our haunted house ready." "That's plenty of time," Tony said. "We can whip this thing together by next weekend!"

I shook my head. "Not when you think about all of the other things that have to be done," I said. "First off, this place is going to need a good cleaning. We also have to make some flyers and put them up around town. And we have to make tickets for people to buy."

"Parker's right," Shane said. "Plus, we have to make

sure that all of the things in the haunted house work just like we want them to. After all . . . we want people to be scared. They aren't going to be scared if we don't do a good job with our spooky effects. Let's get back to work."

We spent the next hour going over the old schoolhouse. I walked around with Holly to get a feel for the rooms. Tony and Dylan went around to find out where they could hide things: they looked for places where they would be able to pull a string and make a rubber spider fall down, or a closet where one of us could jump out and surprise someone. There were lots of tiny crawlspaces and crannies to explore, and we knew we'd found the perfect place for a haunted house.

And we had fun. The schoolhouse no longer seemed so spooky. I was no longer afraid of being around it, or even inside of it. Shane and Lyle laughed a lot as they planned different gags and gadgets to scare people. We'd become comfortable in the old schoolhouse, forgetting all about ghosts and ghoulies and Reginald Perrywinkle.

But not for long.

12

Days flew by. When we weren't in school, we spent every spare moment working out ideas and putting things together for our haunted house. Just cleaning and dusting the inside of the schoolhouse took an entire day, even with six of us working together. Tony and Dylan rigged up a network of fishing lines that ran to the ceiling and spread throughout the schoolhouse. Each line did something different, and Tony was in charge of it all. When he pulled on one line, a giant rubber bat swooped down in the hall, suspended by a different line altogether.

He had to work really hard to get the bat to dip down low enough to be seen, but not so low as to hit any of our unsuspecting customers. There was a line connected to a huge, basketball-sized spider. He could easily maneuver the spider up and down by pulling on the line, letting it back up, then pulling it again. He even had a line that was connected to a rubber skeleton that hung at the bottom of the basement steps. When our customers went downstairs, Tony would turn a crank really fast. The skeleton would 'attack' the people on the stairs. This was another effect that he worked tirelessly on so that it would be really scary. He tried it out on me, and I freaked out—even though I knew what he had been working on. He had borrowed the rubber skeleton from a science teacher from school, and man . . . did it look real.

There were other things, too. Holly strung phony spider web all over the halls, the classrooms and the basement. We hung a big cloth pumpkin banner above the front door of the school, which looked great. We carved pumpkins and placed them on the floor near the walls. We decided not to use candles inside of them, since there were so many and we were indoors. The *last* thing we needed was a fire . . . we'd already had an experience with that (two experiences, if you count the blaze that burned Shane's garage, where we used to hold our meetings before we built a clubhouse) and we all knew that fire wasn't something you mess around with. So we bought a bunch of those little bendable glow sticks. They come in different colors, and they glow for several hours. Actually, they worked better than candles because they weren't as bright. The colorful, glowing pumpkins cast eerie shadows in the basement.

But the best thing in the basement was the coffin that sat in the middle of the room. Shane and Lyle had built it out of scrap wood and painted it black. They drilled a tiny peephole near the front. The plan was simple, but effective. Lyle would dress up like a mummy, lay down in the coffin, and close the lid. While inside, he could look out the peephole to see if anyone was around. When a customer got close to the coffin, Lyle would push the lid open and rise up. It was awesome! When Lyle gave us a demonstration, we clapped and cheered.

Dollar wandered the old schoolhouse on his own, watching us curiously. Sometimes, he would curl up in a corner and sleep.

"Hey, Shane," Tony said, as we gathered in the hall of the old schoolhouse one afternoon. "If all of us are in costume, who's going to take tickets?"

"Yeah," Dylan said. "And who's going to let our

customers in and out?"

"I've already thought of that," Shane replied. "My little brother said he'd help, and he's already got three of his friends that will, too. I told them that we'd pay them five dollars for each day."

Dylan was taken aback. "But that's forty dollars for two days!" he protested. "What if we don't even earn that much?"

"It's a chance we have to take," Shane said. "We can't haunt the old schoolhouse unless we have some helpers outside. Besides, like my dad says: you have to spend money to make money. Our biggest problem right now isn't money . . . it's our costumes. We've got to figure out who is going to dress up as what. Lyle, you're going to be a mummy, so that's settled."

"I can be a witch," Holly said, raising her hand. "I have a costume from last year."

"That'll work," Shane said with a nod.

"I can be a vampire," I said. "I'll use my mom's make-up and color my face white. And I can buy a cheap pair of plastic fangs."

"Great," Shane said. "Tony?"

Tony shrugged. "I've still got my werewolf costume from two years ago," he said. "I'm sure it will still fit. I'm not going to wear the mask, though, because it'll be too hot. But I can make up my face to match my costume."

"Perfect," Shane said. "The less money we have to spend on costumes, the better."

"But what about you, Shane?" Holly asked. "What are you going to be?"

"I'm going to dress up as a zombie," he said without hesitation. "I can dress in ratty old clothes and use make-up so my face will look dead. That won't cost any money at all."

"And I'll be a ghost," Dylan said.

"Good," Shane said. We all agreed that Dylan would make a pretty good ghost.

However, when Dylan showed us his costume the next day, we knew right away that it wouldn't work. His costume consisted of nothing more than a sheet that he pulled over his head. He had poked two holes where his eyes were. When he showed us this for the first time, he ran up and down the hallway of the old schoolhouse, waving his arms, shouting *"whooo-ha-ha-ha, whooo-ha-ha-ha!"* at the top of his lungs. He looked pretty goofy.

"Man, you couldn't scare a flea with that thing," Tony said, shaking his head. "You look like a piece of runaway laundry."

Even through his sheet, you could tell that Dylan was disappointed. "Is it really that bad?" he asked.

BREGE

"It's pretty corny," Lyle said flatly. "I mean . . . corny in a *nice* way."

"Too bad you couldn't dress up as the ghost of Reginald Perrywinkle," Holly said.

That was a great idea. After all, everyone in town was familiar with the stories of old man Perrywinkle. It would be fun for people to see his ghost . . . even if it wasn't real.

But Dylan didn't look anything like the old headmaster. Neither did any of us, so the idea was scrapped. We told Dylan to go back to the drawing board and come up with another costume.

However, we also had a bigger problem.

We were exactly one week away from Saturday, October 30th—the day we would open the haunted house—and we still needed one more thing. We needed something that would be our showstopper, something that would make our customers really freak out. It was important to us. Our customers would be paying good money to be scared, and by golly, we wanted to scare them.

But on Monday, something happened that changed everything.

On Monday—five days before our haunted house was set to open—I received a panicky call from Lyle

Haywood. He was frantic and out of breath.

"Parker!" he shrieked into the phone. *"You've got to get here! Fast!"*

"Where?!?!" I asked. "What's wrong?"

"I'm at Dylan's house!" he gasped. *"You've got to get here! Hurry! Dylan's had an accident!"*

13

A knot of fear tightened my stomach.

An accident? I thought. *Dylan? What happened? Was he okay?*

Lyle sure sounded freaked out, and that's not like him at all. To hear his panic-stricken voice made me worry even more.

I hopped on my bike and raced to Dylan's house as fast as I could pedal, arriving at the same time as Shane and Holly. Tony got there a moment later.

Lyle was sitting on the ground near the Bunker's

garage. Dylan's mom drives a blue minivan, and it was parked in the driveway.

But Dylan was nowhere in sight.

"What's wrong?" Holly shouted, as we approached Lyle. All of us were panting and out of breath.

"What's happened to Dylan?" Shane asked, as his bike skidded to a stop. "Is he all right?"

"He's all right," Lyle said, getting to his feet. "He just had an accident, that's all. Come on out, Dylan."

What's going on? I wondered. *What kind of accident had Dylan had?*

Suddenly, Dylan came out of the garage—and he was completely white! Every inch of his body was covered in a white powdery substance.

"Hi, guys," he said sheepishly.

"Dylan . . . what happened to you?" Holly asked.

"I was helping my mom unload groceries," he replied. "Lyle was here, and he was helping, too. Mom bought a big bag of flour and asked me to put it on a shelf in the garage until she could make room for it in the kitchen. The only shelf where it would fit was over my head. I tried to shove it up there, but—"

"But the thing broke open," Lyle interrupted, "and spilled flour all over him."

"But are you all right?" I asked.

"I'm fine," Dylan replied with a shrug.

"Then what's the big deal?" Tony snarled. "I was in the middle of playing basketball. I came over here because of *this?!?!*"

"Think about it, guys," Lyle said with a wide grin. He pointed at Dylan. "What does he look like?"

"He looks like a ghost," Shane said.

When Shane said 'ghost', it was like a firecracker went off.

"Oh my gosh!" Holly exclaimed. "You *do* look like a ghost!"

"Not only that," Lyle said, his excitement growing, "just think about it! We give Dylan a phony beard and mustache, slick his hair back, pour flour all over him, place him in the chair behind the desk in the headmaster's office, and *bingo!* We've got the ghost of Reginald Perrywinkle, right here, right now!"

"Lyle!" Shane exclaimed. "That's brilliant! I'll bet we can make Dylan look *exactly* like Perrywinkle!"

What a stroke of luck! Here we were, less than a week from our opening day, and we'd come up with the *perfect* showstopper for our haunted house. For years, people have told stories about the ghost of Reginald Perrywinkle.

Now they were going to see him, up close and

personal . . . courtesy of Dylan Bunker and the Adventure Club.

We worked every single day, practicing our gimmicks and gags until everything was perfect. Shane used money from our club treasury and bought a fake beard and mustache at a department store in Cheboygan, which is a city about ten miles north of Great Bear Heart. He also bought a bag of flour at the Great Bear Heart Market, and we had Dylan go through a 'dress rehearsal' on Thursday. We wanted to make sure that his costume would work like we wanted it to.

Tony had an old black light that he bought at a garage sale. He thought it would be cool to use in the headmaster's office. Problem was, there was no electricity in the old schoolhouse. Lyle solved the problem by running a long extension cord out an air vent in the headmaster's office, down the outside wall, and over to a nearby house. The guy who owned the house said that he could plug the extension cord into an outlet in the garage.

And the black light was perfect! We set it up under the desk, and Dylan, covered in flour, glowed an eerie blue-green color in the mysterious light. If he kept his face stern and didn't smile, he could easily pass for the ghost of Reginald Perrywinkle.

"Man, you look awesome!" Shane said to Dylan, who was seated behind the desk. "You look just like him!"

"Question is," Tony said, "can you stay in character all day long?"

Dylan nodded slowly. "Of course!" he said in his best gruff voice. "Once I'm here, I'll be Reginald Perrywinkle all day long!" He raised his arm, scowled, and pointed an accusing finger. "I'm Headmaster Perrywinkle!" he growled. "I've come back to haunt you!"

"Perfect!" Tony exclaimed. I had to admit, Dylan really *did* look like the old headmaster. I was sure he was going to give a lot of people more than a few scares.

Shane had a portable stereo system that was battery-operated. We set it up at the end of the hall near the headmaster's office and covered it with dried corn stalks. Tony had a compact disc with creepy music and sounds, and we'd play it while customers wandered through the old schoolhouse.

Holly designed tickets on her computer, and printed them. Lyle suggested that we have advance ticket sales at the market and the hardware store, which sounded like a good idea. He said we should charge one dollar for tickets in advance, and a dollar twenty-five for each ticket sold at the door. Shane and Tony talked with George

Bloomer at the market, and he said that he'd be happy to sell the tickets there. Holly and I went to the hardware store and asked the owner, Mr. Farnell, if he would sell tickets for us, and he said he would. We left Mr. Farnell with one hundred tickets, the same amount that Shane and Tony had left at the market.

We were all set for our weekend of haunting, and we knew that we were going to have a lot of fun—and earn a lot of money, too.

And that's when the really weird things started to happen.

14

Saturday morning . . . our first day.

Lyle, Shane, Holly, and I arrived at the old schoolhouse that morning at ten and got into costume. Our haunting officially began at noon, and we wanted to be sure that we were ready.

I must say that I was a bit nervous. I think we all were, but we didn't talk about it. There was a gnawing in the back of my mind that had grown stronger and stronger over the past few days.

What if nobody comes? I thought. *What if we don't earn*

any money at all?

I knew that we'd done everything we could. We had put together a really cool haunted house. We'd put up flyers all over town, and told our friends at school.

Still, we didn't know if anybody would show up. We had no idea if we'd earn any money at all . . . until Tony Gritter came riding up on his bicycle that Saturday morning. He leapt off and let the bike fall to the ground.

"Guys!" he shouted. *"All the tickets sold out!"*

"What?!?!" Shane exclaimed.

"It's true!" Tony continued, out of breath. "I just stopped by the Great Bear Heart Market to see how ticket sales were going. They sold all one hundred tickets!"

He dug into the pocket of his denim jeans and pulled out a huge wad of paper bills. "One hundred smackeroonies! And the hardware store sold out, too!" He dug into his other pocket and pulled out yet another wad. "One hundred *more!*"

"Plus," Holly said excitedly, "we'll get customers who don't have tickets and will pay at the door!"

We all cheered. Our haunted house had been a total success . . . and we hadn't even officially opened for business.

BREGE

"Okay, okay," Shane said. "Let's just make sure that we give our customers every penny's worth."

I couldn't believe that we sold out both at the market and the hardware store. That would mean that we would have at least two hundred people coming to walk through our haunted house over a two-day period . . . and maybe more. Like Holly said, more people would probably show up and buy their tickets at the door.

Shane's little brother and his three friends arrived, and we showed them everything they needed to do. Two of them would be at the front door, taking and selling tickets, while the other two worked the back door, letting people out as they departed. After one round of customers had left, one of the kids at the back door would go inside and ring the school bell once, alerting the two helpers in the front that we were ready for our next group of visitors.

And we brought sandwiches, snacks, and bottled water. After all, we wouldn't be able to take any lunch breaks once we got started. I packed two sandwiches and some candy bars, along with a bottle of water and a bottle of lemonade, and put them on the floor in the closet where I would be hiding. That way, I could snack without having to go off the job.

"Where's Dylan?" Shane asked, as we all got ready to

take our positions.

"He'll be here," Lyle said. "You know Dylan. He's always late."

"He'd better not be late this morning," Tony grumbled. "People might start showing up any minute. He's an important part of our haunted house."

"Let's just get ourselves ready," I said. "Dylan will make it here in time. He always comes through."

Sure enough, while we were making final preparations, Dylan came through the back door of the schoolhouse. He was already decked out, completely covered with flour, and he looked just like old Reginald Perrywinkle.

"Great job!" I said to him, as I stepped into my hiding place in the closet. "You're going to freak every—"

Shane's voice suddenly echoed through the old schoolhouse, stopping me in mid-sentence. *"Places, everyone!"* he shouted. *"We've got customers coming!"*

Dylan disappeared into the headmaster's office. I ducked into the closet and closed the door.

The haunting of the old schoolhouse on Oak Street was about to begin . . . in ways that we hadn't planned.

15

To say that things went great would be an understatement.

Things went *fantastic*.

Of course, from where I was in the closet, I couldn't tell exactly what was going on. The door was cracked open a tiny bit, and I couldn't see much. So, when I saw a shadow walk by, I flung the door open and scared the living daylights out of whoever was there. Everybody jumped and screamed, then they laughed and kept on moving. I ducked back into the closet and waited for my next round of victims.

And it was like that throughout the schoolhouse. While I waited in the darkness of the closet, I could hear people scream and shout throughout the building. The spooky music and sound effects were great, and they only enhanced the horror.

And when people filed by the headmaster's office, they shrieked! I could hear Dylan every once in a while, talking in a deep, gruff voice. "What are you doing here?!?!" he would say. "Get out! Get out now!" He played his part perfectly.

All day long, customers came and went. I lost track of time, but I didn't care. In between scaring people, I nibbled on my sandwiches and sipped my bottled water, so I didn't get hungry or thirsty.

But there was one thing we didn't plan on, and it affected all of us. We thought we were ready for everything—water, food, emergencies . . . but we didn't include one important thing:

Bathroom breaks.

Oh, man! By the time we closed our haunted house at eight o'clock, I thought I was going to die. When our helpers at the back door shouted that our last customers of the day were gone, I burst from the closet and headed for the front door. I ran into Lyle Haywood as he bounded up the basement stairs, still in his mummy costume. I almost knocked him over.

"Man, I really gotta go!" he exclaimed.

"Me, too!" I said, and we raced out the front door of the schoolhouse and ran down the steps.

And we weren't the only ones, either. Tony was already on his bike, speeding off. Holly, still in her witch costume, was way ahead of me, running to her house. Our four helpers had disappeared, too.

Later, I called Shane. We'd all left in a hurry, and I wanted to make sure that the schoolhouse was locked up for the night.

"I went back and locked it up," he said. "But let's meet a little earlier tomorrow morning. We'll need to clean things up a bit before our customers get there. You call Holly and Dylan and let them know. I'll call Tony and Lyle."

I hung up and dialed Holly's number. Holly's mom said that she was getting cleaned up, but she would give her the message. I hung up, called Dylan's house, and got the answering machine, which wasn't surprising. Dylan's mom works on Saturday nights, and his dad spends the weekends in his garage workshop. Dylan was probably in the shower, cleaning off six pounds of flour.

I left him a message to be at the old schoolhouse early Sunday, that we'd have some cleaning to do in addition to getting ready for the last day of our haunted house.

I went to bed, but I had a hard time falling asleep. The day had been so much fun! First, Tony showed up with all that money. The haunting had been a complete success, with lots of screams and shrieks and laughs. I think all of our customers enjoyed themselves and thought that a trip through our haunted house was well worth the money they spent. I felt really good. We worked hard, and we earned every penny of what we'd made . . . and we'd earn even *more* tomorrow.

Which happened to be October 31st.

Halloween.

Now, we had *thought* everything had gone according to our plans. Our haunting had been perfect, without any glitches or problems.

But just because we *thought* things had gone according to plan, didn't mean they had.

We were about to find out the truth about the ghost of Reginald Perrywinkle.

16

Honestly, we didn't realize that anything was wrong. We thought that our haunted schoolhouse was a complete success . . . until it was all over.

It was Halloween, and our second and final day of the haunted schoolhouse. It was warm, and we were comfortable in our costumes, except for Tony. He said his werewolf costume was too hot, even without the mask. Dylan was late again, and Shane was getting mad.

"Didn't you call him last night?" he asked me.

"Yeah," I replied, "I did. No one answered the phone, so I left a message for him on the machine."

Customers began arriving at eleven-thirty, and there still was no sign of Dylan. At eleven forty-five, I spotted him wandering behind the school, near the playground.

"Dylan!" I exclaimed. "Where have you been?!?!"

He stopped walking and pointed at me. "I've come back to haunt you!" he hissed.

"Yeah, well, you'd better get to haunting your office!" I shot back. "People are starting to line up!"

I found Shane at the front of the schoolhouse. "Dylan's here," I told him.

"Finally!" Shane said. "Now we can get started!"

The nice weather brought out even more customers than the day before, and everything worked just as planned. I think I jumped out of my closet a hundred times!

And we were a little smarter on Halloween, too, taking a ten-minute bathroom break for all of us at exactly four o'clock. There was a line of people waiting to get in to our haunted house, so we went out the back door. Dylan must've really had to go, because he was already gone by the time the rest of us shuffled out.

We returned and waited by the front and back doors, while Shane's little brother and his friends ran home to take a break.

"Just a few more minutes, folks," Shane said to the

people standing in line. The ticket-takers returned a few minutes later, and our haunting continued.

Daylight faded, and still more people came. Cars lined the street, since the small dirt parking lot was already filled. At one time, the line of people stretched all the way through the lot and along Great Bear Heart Mail Route Road. At eight o'clock, I had no idea how many customers we'd had over the course of the day. In fact, we had to stay open a little after eight: there was still a line of people waiting to go through, and we wanted to make sure everyone got a chance to experience our haunted schoolhouse.

When the last small group had exited, I opened the closet door, slipped out, walked down the hall, and downstairs to the basement. The sun had vanished over an hour ago, and it was dark outside.

Orange pumpkins glowed different colors, giving off the only light. Lyle the Mummy had emerged from the coffin, and he stood next to Shane the Zombie, talking.

"That was awesome!" I said. "I can't believe how many customers we had!"

Holly came down the steps, followed by Shane's little brother and his friends. One of the kids handed us a shoe box filled with ticket stubs and money. Like we'd hoped, there had been a lot of people who showed up and bought their tickets at the door.

A flashlight beam lit up the stairs and Tony came down, looking frighteningly good in his werewolf costume.

"What a great day!" he exclaimed.

"Bring that light over here," Shane said, "so we can pay our helpers and they can go home."

Shane counted out some money and handed a small wad to each of the four kids. "I gave you each an extra two dollars for doing such good work," he said.

The kids were thrilled. In the glow of the pumpkins, they stared at the money in their hands, mesmerized. Shane had given each of them twelve dollars.

"That's more money than I've ever made in my life!" one kid said.

"Yeah!" one of the other kids chirped. "If you ever need any more help for anything, let us know!"

We thanked them and they shuffled off, climbed the stairs, and left. We heard them whooping and hollering all the way down the street, rushing off to go trick-or-treating before it got too late.

"Where's Dylan?" Holly asked.

"I saw him go out the back door," Tony said. "He didn't even say anything to me."

"He probably wants to get that flour off as soon as

he can," Shane said. "Being covered in that stuff all day was probably uncomfortable."

"Let's count the money!" Lyle said.

Shane shook his head. "Holly, you're the club treasurer. You take the money home and bring it back here tomorrow after school. I promised the township supervisor that we'd leave the place cleaner than we found it, but it's getting too late to do it tonight. "

We agreed to meet after school the next day.

"We sure scared and surprised a lot of people," Holly said, as the five of us climbed the steps, turned, and walked outside. Tony paused, however, grabbing the bell rope.

"And one more ring of the schoolhouse bell to mark the end of a successful haunting," he said.

He pulled the rope.

Nothing happened.

No *bong!*

Nothing.

He tugged again, harder this time.

Still nothing.

"It must be caught on something," Tony said, shining his light up. However, since the rope disappeared into the ceiling, we couldn't see what was wrong.

"Forget about it," Shane said. "It's probably stuck.

We can check it out tomorrow, during the daylight."

We went our separate ways, except for Holly and me. We walked down the street together, talking and laughing about the days' events. There were still a few trick-or-treaters wandering about, rushing from house to house with their bags of goodies swinging. In a way, I missed not being able to trick-or-treat . . . but there was always next year.

The wind hissed through the trees. Oak and maple leaves, brown and brittle, scraped along the pavement like fingernails on a blackboard. When I stepped on them, they crunched like potato chips.

"I bet we scared a billion people," I said.

"Everyone had a good time, I think," Holly offered. "I know *I* did."

We stopped at my driveway, where a small shadow darted from the brush and ran up to us. Holly, instinctively knowing what it was, knelt down and scooped up Dollar in her arms.

"Hi, little buddy," she said, as the cat snuggled up to her neck.

"I'll see you tomorrow," I said, and I turned to walk to my house.

"Parker?" Holly said.

I stopped and turned around. It was dark, and all I

could see was her silhouette a few feet in front of me. I didn't say anything, and she spoke again.

"Did you . . . did . . . oh, forget it. I'll see you tomorrow."

"What?" I asked. "Did I what?"

"Well . . . I can't help but feel that something just isn't right. I . . . I mean . . . *wasn't* right these past two days. I don't know . . . but while we were in the schoolhouse, something just didn't seem . . . it didn't seem *right.* Did you feel it?"

"No," I said, shaking my head. "I didn't feel anything."

But as I turned and walked away, I had a knot in my stomach that hurt.

It hurt because I hadn't told Holly the truth.

I *had* felt something at the schoolhouse. I didn't know what it was, or where it came from, but Holly was right.

Something about the old schoolhouse just wasn't *normal.*

And before sundown the next day, we all would know what it was.

17

Monday, November 1st.

The old schoolhouse.

We met after school, just as Shane had ordered. I was dressed in a pair of old jeans and a heavy flannel shirt, ready to begin our clean-up. Tony was wearing a pair of beige coveralls and a heavy T-shirt, and Lyle had on a pair of stained blue jeans and a *University of Michigan* sweatshirt. Holly showed up wearing jeans and a sweatshirt, carrying Dollar in her arms. Shane looked just like Tony, except his sweatshirt read *I'm a Jenius.*

Everyone was there . . . except for Dylan Bunker.

He wasn't just *late* . . . he didn't show at all. We all waited and waited, thinking that he would show up sooner or later.

But he didn't.

Finally, after a half an hour waiting, we decided that we'd better get started cleaning . . . with or without Dylan.

And it was hard work. The spider web that we'd used to decorate the inside of the school was messy, and it was hard to clean up. We spent hours removing pumpkins, retrieving the fishing lines that Tony had laid out around the building, and picking up our props. The coffin in the basement was heavy, and it took all of us to carry it upstairs. Lyle ran home and returned with a wagon, and we placed the coffin on it. Lyle pulled the wagon while Shane and Tony walked alongside, balancing the coffin so it didn't fall. They took it to Tony's house and came back a few minutes later to help finish cleaning. It was nearly seven o'clock before we were done.

"And that little red-haired weasel never showed up," Tony spat. "Some friend he is."

"I didn't see him in school today," I said. "I looked for him, but I couldn't find him."

"Maybe we can make him pay extra dues next month," Lyle suggested.

Holly spoke. "Something's wrong, you guys," she said.

"What do you mean?" Shane asked.

Holly looked around. "Okay," she said. "Nobody lie. Parker . . . this means *you.*"

I felt as tall as a mouse as Holly looked me square in the eyes.

"You knew that something wasn't right about these past two days, didn't you?" she asked. "I asked you last night, but you wouldn't admit it."

I didn't say anything.

"Didn't anyone else feel it?" Holly asked accusingly, looking around at each of us. "Am I the only one? Or am I the only one that's being honest?"

"Holly's right," I said, finally. "I had a weird feeling this whole weekend, but I just didn't say anything."

Lyle Haywood hung his head. "Me too," he said. "I felt something the whole time we were here. It felt like . . . like—"

"—like we didn't belong," Holly finished for him. "Like we shouldn't have been here."

Even Tony agreed. "I was going to say something on that very first night," he said, "right after I rang the bell. I did it to scare you guys. But something scared me a *lot* more than it did you . . . I just didn't admit it."

"Speaking of which," Shane said, "we never did figure out what was wrong with the bell last night."

"I tried to ring it again," Tony said, "just a few minutes ago. Nothing happened."

"Something's up with that," I said. "Let's check out the bell and find out what's wrong. I hope we didn't break it."

"The guy that let us plug in our extension cord has a ladder," Lyle said. "Let's ask if we can borrow it."

And that's what we did. The five of us walked over to the house next door. His garage was open, and a single light bulb burned above his car. The vehicle's hood was up, and the man was working on the engine.

"Hi, guys," he said, as we approached. "How did your haunted house go?"

"Great," Shane said, stepping into the garage. "But we were wondering if we could borrow your ladder."

The man peered out from beneath the hood. "Sure . . . but what for?"

"We think we might have broken the bell," Tony said. "We just want to take a look."

The man looked at Tony, then laughed. "Well, I don't see how you could have broken it," he said. "That bell has been gone for years."

"No, it hasn't," Holly said. "We used it all weekend.

Our helpers rang it to let us know that another group of customers was coming through."

"All weekend, eh?" the man said. "I've been here all weekend, and I didn't hear a thing."

"You must have," I said. "I heard it. We *all* heard it."

"Boys," the man said, and then he glanced at Holly, "and *lady*. That bell was removed in 1970. It used to ring all by itself, in the middle of the night. Everyone said that it was the ghost of Reginald Perrywinkle, ringing the bell to scare everyone."

My skin crawled as a chill went down my spine.

"They removed the bell and took it down to the historical museum," the man continued, "and that's where it is to this day. There hasn't been a bell in that old schoolhouse in over thirty years."

"This guy is out of his mind," Tony whispered to me. *"I heard the bell. So did you. So did everyone."*

"Well, could we borrow the ladder anyway?" Shane asked. "Just to see for ourselves?"

"I don't see why not," the man said, pointing to his garage. "Help yourself."

The ladder was leaning against the wall on the inside of the garage. Tony and Shane picked it up and carried it outside. They walked across the grass and stood it up at the front of the steps. In two seconds, Tony was scrambling up the ladder on his way to the bell tower.

"What do you see?" Holly asked.

"It's too dark," he said. "I can't see through the boards."

"Catch," Shane said, reaching into his sweatshirt pocket and pulling out his flashlight. He tossed the light into the air, and Tony caught it in his right hand. He switched it on and aimed the beam through the wooden slats.

"Oh, man!" he said. *"The guy next door is right! There's no bell here!"*

Now, *that* was freaky. Horrifying, in fact.

And it was about to get worse.

18

Tony came down from the ladder. When he stood on the ground, he was shaking. Now, as I've said, Tony Gritter is a pretty tough guy. Oh, he wouldn't hurt anyone . . . unless someone was hurting him or one of his friends. Tony just isn't a guy who gets scared easily.

But it was easy to see that he was scared now. Somehow . . . whatever the reason . . . the bell rang all weekend, whenever the rope was pulled. Now we found out that the bell was removed over thirty years ago!

It didn't make any sense.

"Let's go to Dylan's house," I suggested.

"Something's wrong with him, too. It's not like him not to show up. I mean . . . he's always late, but he always gets here."

"Parker's right," Holly said. "Let's go over to his house."

Shane locked up the old school, and we walked down the quiet street toward Dylan's house. Leaves were everywhere. Some swirled at our feet, some were still tethered tenuously to their limbs, crackling in the chilly October breeze. A layer of clouds kidnapped the stars and the moon, but the intermittent streetlights led our way to the Bunker home. Dollar scampered at Holly's heels.

It was seven-thirty. Night had fallen, and there were lights on in the house. And, of course, the lights in the Bunker's garage lit up the building like a spacecraft. Dylan's dad spent hours and hours there, working on different projects.

We strode up the walk and onto the porch. The Bunker's have a motion-activated light that turns on when something moves nearby, and the porch light automatically blinded us. I mean . . . it was *bright!* We all raised our arms to shield our eyes from the glare.

Lyle reached out and pressed the doorbell. We heard a faint, muffled *ding-dong*. A shadow appeared through the curtain, and the door opened. Mrs. Bunker stood in the doorway, wearing an apron that had a ghost and a cat stitched on it. She was holding a large spoon, and I could smell the sweet, heavy scent of pumpkin pie drifting through the open door.

"Why, hello," she said with a smile. "This is so very nice of you."

I didn't know what she meant by that, but it didn't matter.

"Mrs. Bunker . . . is Dylan home?" Shane asked.

"Why, of course he is," Mrs. Bunker replied.

"Can we talk to him?" Lyle asked.

"Oh, I don't think that would be a very good idea," she replied. "You know . . . considering."

"Considering *what?"* Holly asked.

"Well, the flu, of course," Mrs. Bunker answered. "Isn't that why you're here? To see how he's doing?"

We were dumbfounded.

"You . . . you mean that Dylan is *sick?"* I asked.

Mrs. Bunker nodded. "He came down with the flu on Friday night," she said, very concerned-like. "He hasn't left his bed since."

We looked at each other with puzzled expressions.

"Since *Friday night,* Mrs. Bunker?" Shane asked.

"Yes, that's right," Mrs. Bunker replied with a nod.

"Since Friday night. The doctor says that until Dylan recovers, he shouldn't leave his bed. Dylan has been home all weekend."

I looked at Holly. Holly looked at Tony. Tony looked at Lyle. Lyle looked at Shane, who was looking at me. Then we exchanged glances, and I could see the terror building in everyone's faces. All five of us were freaked. All five of us were confused. All five of us wondered—

If Dylan Bunker had been sick all weekend, then who had been in the headmaster's office for two days in a row?

19

One week later, in our clubhouse.

Dylan Bunker was feeling better, and he was able to attend our meeting. He was fifteen minutes late, of course, but none of us cared. He'd been really sick, and we were just glad that he was feeling well enough to venture out.

Of course, we were still talking about what had happened at the old schoolhouse. The bell, indeed, was at the Great Bear Heart Historical Museum. Holly and I had seen it for ourselves when we went to investigate.

The real mystery, and perhaps the scariest part of the whole weekend, was the fact that Dylan was sick and had remained in bed . . . yet, we'd all seen the ghostly white figure seated in the headmaster's room.

"You know," Shane said, "I can't remember speaking to Dylan the whole weekend. At least, who I *thought* was Dylan."

"I talked to him, but he didn't say much to me," I said. "I just thought it was Dylan, staying in character."

"I was so sick I almost puked on my dog," Dylan said. "I didn't go anywhere. Mom got the message that Parker called, but I was too sick to call anybody back."

"There's only one person it could have been," Holly said.

"No," Lyle said, "not a person. A *thing*. A ghost."

We were silent. The wind caused our clubhouse to gently sway within the giant limbs of the maple. A few brown, curled leaves found their way through the open windows, falling to the floor. Through the window, I could see dozens of them twisting and flipping through the air beneath a curtain of gray sky. A skein of Canadian geese flew in a V-shaped formation, migrating south for the winter. We listened to their lonely honking until they vanished from sight.

And that was that. We never again talked about what had happened that weekend. Oh, we talked about how we'd made a haunted house, and how we earned nearly three hundred dollars. We laughed at how we'd scared and surprised our customers, and how cool the old schoolhouse looked after we'd decorated it.

But we never spoke of the ghost of Reginald Perrywinkle, or how the old bell rang . . . when it wasn't even there.

And we never again set foot in the old schoolhouse on Oak Street.

November came, and the nights grew colder. When I got up in the morning, everything was covered with a fuzzy, silver dew. There was no snow on the ground yet, but we knew it was on its way. At our weekly meetings, we talked about some of the fun things we could do over the winter. After all, we had quite a bit of money, and we put our heads together to decide the best way to spend it. What we really wanted was an ice boat, which is a really cool one-person sailboat-type craft that is used on frozen lakes during the winter. They go really fast when it's windy, and we thought that it would be fun to buy one and take turns with it on Puckett Lake. Unfortunately, they cost a lot of money—a lot more than we had, as a matter of fact—and we knew that there was no way we'd have enough to buy one this year.

Until Tony Gritter got an idea to earn even *more* money than what we'd made with our haunted house.

A *lot* more money.

We were in our clubhouse for what would be one of the last meetings here until spring. Oh, we'd still get together, but it was too dangerous to use our clubhouse after the snow fell. The rope ladder would be too slippery, and we didn't want to risk falling. So, during the winter months, we would take turns meeting in each other's houses.

"Look," Tony said, pulling out a yellow and black paperback book. I recognized it instantly as *The Old Farmer's Almanac.* It's a book of predictions and facts and things that's published once a year.

"This winter," Tony continued, flipping through the pages, "is supposed to be one of the worst winters ever. Tons and tons of snow!"

"Cool!" Dylan said.

"Yeah," I said. "Maybe we'll have a few more snow days." In the winter, Great Bear Heart can get a lot of snow. When it snows more than ten inches in one night, or if the roads get really slick, school usually gets cancelled.

"I've got an idea," Tony said. "A way we can make a pile of money!"

"How's that?" Shane asked.

"We use the season to our advantage," Tony replied.

"The more snow we get, the more money we can earn!"

Tony explained his idea, and we all agreed: we could earn a *lot* of money.

And one thing we were about to learn: there's no business like snow business.

THERE'S NO BUSINESS LIKE SNOW BUSINESS

1

Tony Gritter had an idea . . . and after we thought about it, we admitted that he might be on to something.

Something *big.*

"Think about it," he said. "We can earn money by shoveling snow. Everybody has to shovel snow, right?"

We nodded. You see, when a lot of snow falls in Great Bear Heart, it falls *everywhere.* On houses, in the forest, in fields . . . and in *driveways.* When there is a lot of snow, you have to move it before you drive a car on it. Otherwise, the vehicle might get stuck, especially if it's not a four-wheel drive.

"That's what our job will be!" Tony continued excitedly. "We can earn money by shoveling snow from driveways! It's a tough job, and most people don't want to do it. Some people are just too busy."

"Except for the Adventure Club!" Dylan exclaimed. He stood up from the milk crate he'd been seated on and pretended he had a snow shovel, pushing it forward and then throwing it back over his shoulder. "I'm ready! All we need is the snow!"

"We might even earn enough money to buy an ice boat!" I said.

We took a vote, and, naturally, we all were in favor. Our plan was simple:

Each of us had our own snow shovels, so we could start working without spending any money for equipment. We really didn't have to do anything else to prepare . . . except wait.

We kept careful watch of the weather reports. Finally, in the first week of December, we got word that a snowstorm was coming. It was going to be a good one, too, with over six inches of snow predicted.

"Okay," Shane said one afternoon when we were gathered in Holly's living room to hold our meeting. "We've got four days before the first storm hits. Let's see if we can get some customers ahead of time."

"Ahead of time?" Dylan asked. He scratched his head. "But there isn't even any snow on the ground."

"That's right," Shane said. "Here's the deal: everybody knows the storm is coming. Everybody knows they'll have to get their driveway shoveled. If we go out and drum up some business ahead of time, we might be able to book a few jobs in advance."

"Kind of like taking orders," I said.

"Exactly," Shane said. "And, if for some reason it *doesn't* snow, our customers won't be out any money, because we won't get paid until the job is done."

"How much are we going to charge?" Lyle asked.

Good question.

"Well, let's think about it," Shane said. "Some people have little driveways, some people have big ones. How about charging five dollars for small driveways, and ten dollars for big ones?"

We thought about it for a moment.

"That sounds fair," Holly said.

"Yeah, as long as it's not two feet of snow," Tony said. "That would be a lot of work for ten dollars."

"We can always change our fees," Shane said. "We just have to make sure that we're fair. We don't want to charge anyone too much, but we want to charge enough to make it worth our while."

"Is there anyone else in Great Bear Heart that has a snow shoveling business?" I asked.

Shane shook his head. "Not that I know of," he said. "There are some guys who plow with their trucks, but they charge more than what we'll be charging. We'll be doing the same job as the snow plows, but we'll be charging less. Plus, there are a few other things we can offer to make people want to hire us."

"Like what?" Holly asked. Dollar the cat had wandered into the living room and jumped up into her lap. The cat was asleep almost immediately.

"Well, we can salt people's walkways and porches for no additional charge," he said.

That seemed like a good idea. During the winter, lots of people spread rock salt on their driveways, sidewalks, and porches to melt the ice and to keep it from building up. And the salt provided some traction, making it safer to walk on.

"Where would we get the salt?" Dylan asked.

"We can buy it in fifty pound bags from the Great Bear Heart Market," Shane said. "It's not very expensive."

The plan sounded good. On days that it snowed a lot, we would get up early, meet at the market, and head out together to shovel out our customers' driveways . . . if, of course, we had any. Our first job was to go out before the first storm of the year hit and see if we could find people to hire us. We were excited and hopeful, but, as the saying goes: *nothing ever goes as planned.*

It sure wouldn't go as planned for us.

2

The next day, we met at the Great Bear Heart Market. From there, we planned to head out to find customers.

Shane had ordered all of us to bring snow shovels and carry them over our shoulders, although there wasn't any snow on the ground. "It makes us look ready," he said. "Remember: we want everybody to know that we're prepared."

Lyle Haywood made up some business cards on his computer. They looked really professional, and he gave a handful to each of us.

"These are great!" Tony exclaimed, as he inspected a card. He held it up and read aloud: *"The Adventure Club Snow Shoveling Company - the hardest working kids in snow business. One call does it all!"*

"That's perfect!" Holly said. "I've never had my very own business card!"

"Just to make things easy, I only put Shane's telephone number on the cards," Lyle explained. "It'll be easier for our customers to remember."

We decided to split into groups of two. That way, we could go door-to-door and cover a lot more houses in a shorter period of time.

"And don't forget," Shane said, just before we paired off, "make sure you leave everyone with a card, even if they're not interested. They might change their mind if we get a lot of snow, and they'll call us. Let's meet back here at the market in an hour."

Tony and Lyle headed up the bluff that wound above the highway and looked out over the lake. Dylan and I headed for Oak Street, where we would wind our way behind town. Shane and Holly headed south, covering the area along the highway and the lakeshore, all the way down to *Rollers,* a popular bar and grill.

"What are we going to say to people?" Dylan asked as we trudged up the hill, heading for our first house.

"We hand them a card and warn them about the coming snowstorm," I replied. "Then we ask if they'd like to hire us to shovel their driveway if we get a bunch of snow."

"What if they say no?" Dylan said. He sounded worried.

"We thank them for their time, and move on to the next house."

We walked up to our first prospect. It was a two-story, white house with green trim and a green front door. I must admit that I was a little nervous as I reached out and rang the doorbell. But I took a deep breath, and waited for the owner to come to the door. We heard footsteps approaching, and suddenly, the door swung open. An older man wearing dark slacks and a gray sweater stood in the doorway.

"Yes?" he asked.

"Hello, sir," I said. "I'm Parker Smith, and this is my friend, Dylan Bunker." I handed him a business card.

"We wanna shovel your driveway!" Dylan blurted.

The man looked up from the card and gazed past us and chuckled. "Well, I hate to tell you young fellas this," he began, "but there isn't a snowflake in sight."

"But there will be," I replied, "and soon. And when it comes, you'll need your driveway shoveled."

"How much do you charge?" he asked.

I turned and looked at his driveway. It was long, and I figured that it would be one of the bigger jobs.

"Ten dollars," I said.

"That's not bad," he said. "I'll tell you what. If we get a lot of snow, maybe I'll give you a call."

"Great!" I said. "Call us anytime."

"Yeah!" Dylan said. "We're the hardest working kids in snow business, just like the card says!"

The old man smiled. "You boys have a nice evening. And thank you for stopping by."

"You're welcome," I said, and we left.

House after house, door after door, we couldn't get anyone to hire us. But they all took the card we handed them, and said they'd call if they needed us.

After an hour, we gathered once again at the Great Bear Heart Market. Holly, Shane, Tony, and Lyle hadn't had much success, either. Tony, however, found one lady that said she would definitely hire us.

"It's my aunt," he said with a snicker.

"Fine with me," Shane said. "A job is a job. All we have to do is wait for snow."

"Then we'll get some customers for sure," Holly said. "I know we will."

Well, the weatherman on television had predicted

nearly six inches of snow for the weekend . . . but nobody could have predicted what was about to happen to our business.

3

The snow began falling on Friday afternoon, after I got home from school. The phone rang as I was finishing dinner. It was Holly, and she sounded excited.

"I just got a call from Shane!" she exclaimed. "He says to be on alert!"

"Has he had any phone calls from customers?" I asked.

"Not yet," Holly replied. "But he's sure that if we get all the snow that we're supposed to, we're going to have a busy day tomorrow."

I wasn't so sure. Would people really pay six kids to shovel their driveway? Was ten bucks too much for a big driveway? Too little? I hadn't a clue.

After I hung up the phone, I walked to the window. Even though it was only six-thirty, darkness had fallen. A light glowed from above our garage, and I could see the snow coming down, shifting in the gusting winds. It looked like a thick, white curtain, swaying back and forth.

I hope it keeps up all night, I thought. I crawled into bed, pulled the covers up to my chin, and listened to the howling wind outside my window. Then, I closed my eyes and wished for tons and tons of snow.

And man . . . did I ever get my wish!

I was awakened in the morning by a gentle knock. My bedroom door opened slowly, and my dad popped his head in.

"Hey, Park," he said. "Phone call."

I climbed out of bed and stumbled sleepily down the hall and into the kitchen. My mom was sipping coffee at the table. Dad had been making breakfast, and the smell of bacon and eggs made my mouth water. I plucked the phone from the counter.

"Hello?" I said, and my throat cracked. I was still pretty sleepy.

"Parker! We're in business!"

It was Shane. For a moment, I didn't know what he was talking about.

Then it came to me.

Our snow shoveling business!

"We are?" I said, beginning to wake up.

"Oh, man, are we *ever!*" he exclaimed. "Have you looked outside?"

"Not yet," I replied.

"We've got a foot of new snow! I've already had seven calls! We've got seven customers, and it's only seven o'clock!"

"That's awesome!" I said, slapping the palm of my hand on the counter. Mom and Dad looked at me, wondering what I was so excited about.

"We're all meeting at the market in fifteen minutes," Shane said. "Grab your shovel!"

"See ya!" I said, and I hung up the phone.

"What's all the fuss about?" Mom asked.

"We're going to shovel driveways to earn money!" I proclaimed. "We started a snow shoveling business, and we've already got customers!"

"Good," Dad said. "You can start with *our* driveway."

Rats.

I was late getting to the market, but so was everyone else. As it turned out, I wasn't the only one who had to shovel his own driveway. Tony Gritter's mom made him go to the other side of town and shovel his grandmother's sidewalk.

"But it didn't bother me," he said, rubbing his belly. "She made me sausage and biscuits. Yum!"

"All I had for breakfast was a yogurt," Holly said.

"Geez," Dylan said. "I only had a bowl of cereal."

"Where's Dollar?" I asked Holly.

"I tried to get him to come along, but he took one look at the snow and went back into my bedroom. I don't think he's really thrilled with this weather."

We gathered under the awning outside the Great Bear Heart Market. The snow had stopped. The sky had cleared, and the sun was rising. Thin blades of sunlight sliced through leafless branches, and the morning light on the new-fallen snow made everything look clean and fresh.

Lyle Haywood brought a plastic sled, explaining that it would come in handy for hauling around the fifty pound bag of rock salt. It would be a lot easier to pull the bag around with the sled than to try to carry it.

"I've got the names and addresses of the people who called this morning," Shane said. He dug his gloved hand into his winter coat and pulled out a wrinkled sheet of paper. "Our first customer is on Beagle Street. Mrs. Wallace was the first to call this morning, so we'll start there."

Shane and Tony went into the market to buy a bag of rock salt, and they returned a moment later, each carrying one end of the bag. They were struggling and having a hard time.

"Man," Tony said, "I'm sure glad you brought that sled, Lyle. This stuff weighs a ton!"

They dropped the large sack onto the sled and we set out for Beagle Street, carrying our shovels over our shoulders. Lyle and Dylan pulled the sled through the foot-deep snow.

"Everything looks so pretty," Holly said, looking around. "We sure got a lot of snow last night."

Snow was everywhere. Rooftops looked like they were coated with vanilla frosting. Tree branches sagged from the weight of the snow, and mailboxes appeared to be wearing thick white hats.

When we reached the Wallace's house, we wasted no time. We started shoveling where the driveway met the road, and we didn't stop until we reached the garage. Then, Holly and I shoveled the sidewalk and the porch, while Tony, Lyle, Dylan, and Shane spread handfuls of rock salt on the driveway. It was a big driveway, and it was hard work . . . but with the six of us, the entire job took only about fifteen minutes.

When we finished, we carried our shovels over our

shoulders and walked up to the porch. Shane knocked on the front door, and Mr. Wallace answered. He was an older man, with gray hair and a gray mustache.

"Wow," he said, looking past us and inspecting the driveway. "You kids sure work fast! And you did a good job, too!"

"We're the hardest working kids in snow business!" Dylan said proudly.

"How much do I owe you?" he asked.

"Ten dollars," Shane said.

Mr. Wallace reached into his back pocket and pulled out a black leather wallet. He flipped it open and pulled out a ten-dollar bill.

"Here you go," he said.

Holly took the money and stuffed it in her coat pocket. We thanked Mr. Wallace, and hustled off.

"Ten dollars in fifteen minutes!" Tony exclaimed as we trudged through the snow to our next job. "We're going to be rich!"

"Where to, Shane?" Lyle asked.

Shane pulled out his paper. "Right around the corner, on Chisolm Street," he replied, stuffing the paper back into his coat. "It's—"

He stopped speaking.

Then he stopped walking.

We all stopped.

Coming toward us was Shane's mom, driving their truck. She pulled up slowly and rolled down the window.

And she didn't look happy.

4

"I've been looking all over for you guys!" Mrs. Mitchell said. "The phone has been ringing off the hook!"

"It has?!?!" Shane gasped.

"Yes," Mrs. Mitchell said, "it has. Here's another list of people that want their driveways shoveled." She handed Shane a piece of paper through the open window. "You guys are going to be busy for a while," she said. "If this keeps up, you're going to have to get your own phone line." She smiled, and we relaxed. I thought she was going to be mad, but she wasn't. Then she rolled up the window and drove off slowly in the deep snow.

Shane looked at the list of names and addresses on his new list.

"Holy smokes!" he exclaimed, his breath smokey in the cold temperature. "We've got another eight customers!"

"Your mom is right," Lyle said. "We are going to be busy for a while. We'd better get a move on."

Busy didn't *begin* to explain it.

It took us until lunchtime to finish the driveways on our first list. We didn't even take a break, either. Lunchtime came and went, and we kept going, shoveling driveways and porches. Finally, at three o'clock, we finished our last driveway.

At least, we *thought* we'd finished our last driveway.

Once again, Shane's mom drove up. She was smiling and shaking her head as she rolled down the window.

"More work, guys," she said, handing Shane another list of customers.

We should have been happy, but that wasn't the case. After all . . . we'd been shoveling snow since early in the morning, not even stopping to take a lunch break! We were hungry, tired, and cold.

"Oh, man," Dylan said, spearing his shovel into a snow bank. "I thought we were done!"

"Not anymore," Shane said. "We've got another six

customers."

Tony groaned. "We're all going to be late for dinner," he complained.

"We're going to shovel these driveways," Shane said sternly, "and then we'll eat. If we're late for dinner, that's just the way it goes."

At five-thirty, we finished. The six of us collapsed into a snow bank, exhausted.

"If I see your mother coming, I'm running away," Tony said.

"Me, too," Dylan said. His red hair had looped under his hat and was frozen to the knit fabric. "I'm tired, and I'm starved."

It was getting dark as we got to our feet.

"I'll count the money on Sunday," Holly said, "and we can put it in the bank on Monday."

We used to keep our money in an old coffee can that we hid in the woods. After we made a couple hundred dollars from our haunted schoolhouse, however, we decided it wasn't safe anymore. After all . . . it *was* a lot of money to leave laying around in the forest. So, we voted to open our very own savings account at a bank in Indian River, which was only a few miles away. As club treasurer, it was Holly's responsibility to manage our money in the account. At our weekly meetings, she would report exactly how much we had.

I made it home just in time for dinner, and I told my mom and dad all about our day. Dad thought that our snow shoveling business was a great idea, and he hoped that we earned a lot of money.

After dinner, I took a shower and went straight to bed. It was only seven-thirty, but I was so tired I couldn't keep my eyes open any longer. I'd worked really hard all day, and I was looking forward to a good nights' sleep.

I slept like a baby, all right . . . which was a good thing. Because the phone rang again, early in the morning. Like the previous morning, it was Shane Mitchell calling . . . and I was sure the news was good. I knew that he was calling to tell me that we had a bunch of new customers.

However, Shane did *not* have good news. In fact, it was *terrible* news.

5

Shane called at seven o'clock in the morning, ordering an emergency meeting of the Adventure Club at the Great Bear Heart Market . . . pronto. He sounded bummed out.

"What's wrong?" I asked.

"Just be there, Parker," he said. "I'll explain everything when everyone gets there. And bring your snow shovel."

I hung up, dressed, grabbed a bagel from the kitchen, and chewed it while I put on my boots, hat, coat, and gloves. Thankfully, I was well-rested from my long night of sleep. My muscles were sore and achy from shoveling so much snow the day before, but I felt good and ready for the day.

"More snow shoveling today?" my dad asked. He was at the kitchen table, reading the newspaper as I was putting on my cold weather gear.

"I don't know," I said. "But I think so."

I left my house and hurried through the chilly morning to the Great Bear Heart Market. Dylan was already there, which was strange. He's always late. Tony arrived right after I did, followed by Holly, Shane, and Lyle.

"What's the big deal?" Tony whined. "I wanted to sleep in."

"The big deal is that we've got some angry customers," Shane said.

"What?!?!" Holly exclaimed. "Why?"

"Yeah," Dylan said. "We did a good job. Everybody seemed happy with our shoveling."

"Well," Shane explained, "it seems that after it got dark, some kids went around with shovels and threw a bunch of snow back into the driveways we shoveled."

"What?!?!" Tony exclaimed.

Shane nodded. "I got four calls this morning. One of our customers even accused us of being the ones to pile the snow back into their driveway."

"That's crazy!" Dylan said.

"Yeah," Holly agreed. "Why would we do such a thing?"

Shane continued. "She thought that maybe *we* did it, so we could show up in the morning and try to charge her more money to shovel her driveway again."

"We wouldn't do *that!*" Tony insisted.

Shane shrugged. *"You* know that, and *I* know that," he said, "but maybe our *customers* don't know that."

"There's one thing I *do* know," Tony said. He was fuming. "I bet I know *who* did it! Those lousy Martin brothers!"

Shane held up two gloved hands. "Maybe, maybe not," he said. "The point is, we've got to make sure that our customers are happy. Otherwise, they aren't going to be our customers for very long. We've got to go to their houses and shovel their driveways again."

"Do we get paid?" Dylan asked.

Shane shook his head. "If we charge them again, it might look like we were the ones who threw the snow back in the driveways. They're our customers. We've got to take good care of them, and they need to know it."

Tony doubled up his right fist and slammed it into his left palm. His gloves made a hollow *thunk!* as they smacked together.

"Man, when I see those guys, they're really going to be in for it!" he snapped.

"Hang on, hang on," Shane said. "Like I said: we don't know for sure it was the Martin brothers. There are other kids around that cause trouble."

"Not like those guys," Holly said.

"Shane's right," Lyle said. "The main thing right now is to get those driveways re-shoveled. Let's get going."

It took us almost two hours to re-shovel the driveways. When we finished each driveway, we went to the door and assured our customers that we weren't responsible for pushing the snow into their driveway the night before. They seemed to understand.

All the while, I kept thinking of ways to get even with the Martins. True, we didn't know for certain they had been the ones responsible . . . but the chances were pretty good that they were. Whenever there was mischief in Great Bear Heart, it was a good bet that Terry, Larry, and Gary Martin were probably behind it.

Oh, we've caused a little ruckus ourselves, but we never intentionally did things that would get us or anyone else into trouble.

Not so for the Martin brothers. When it comes to causing trouble, the Martin brothers are professionals. Nobody in Great Bear Heart can make trouble like Gary,

Larry, and Terry Martin.

"Now what?" Dylan asked, as we finished shoveling our last driveway. We were standing by the street, leaning on our snow shovels. It was almost ten o'clock.

"I'll go home and see if any more customers have called," Shane said. "I'll call everybody when I get there."

Tony spoke. "If we don't have any more driveways to shovel, let's go sledding over by Devil's Ridge!"

"Yeah, that would be fun!" Holly said. "Let's do it!"

There is a big hill that's part of Devil's Ridge, which is west of town and back in the woods. There are no houses around at all, and not many people go there. At the bottom of the hill is a creepy old cemetery that we stay away from.

We all went home. Shane phoned and said that no new customers had called. And no one had called to say that someone had shoveled snow back into their driveway . . . for which I was grateful.

"Grab your sled, and meet us at the market after lunch," Shane said.

"See you there," I said. I hung up.

Cool. While I wanted to earn more money shoveling snow, I was still sore from working so hard the day before. Sledding would be a lot more fun.

But, as fate would have it, we weren't the only kids in

Great Bear Heart that decided to go sledding at Devil's Ridge. There were others—three others, to be exact—with the same idea. You guessed it. The Martin brothers. Terry, Larry, and Gary.

Usually, we steered clear of them. Oh, we've had words with them, but, for the most part, we leave them alone. Even in school. We've never had anything more than an argument with them.

This time, however, it was going to be a different story.

6

The six of us gathered at the Great Bear Heart Market, just as Shane had instructed. We all brought our sleds. I have one of those round plastic discs that you sit in. It's really fast, but it's almost impossible to steer. Last winter, I almost crashed! If I hadn't bailed out at the last minute, I would have smacked right into a tree trunk.

Lyle brought the plastic sled that he used to haul the rock salt. Of all our sleds, his was the fastest. Dylan had an old one made out of wood with steel runners. It was way too big for him, but it went pretty fast and was easy to steer. Holly had a wooden toboggan that was big enough for all six of us. Shane and Tony had sleds like

Lyle's, only they were older.

We bought candy bars from the market and stuffed them into our coats, so we'd have something to eat later. It would probably be another long day, and a snack would come in handy.

Devil's Ridge wasn't very far away, but not many people go there. Some are superstitious about the old graveyard. Plus, you can't get there with a car. It's back in the woods, and you have to hike or ride a bike. And in the winter, the snow gets really deep. One year, the snow was so deep that it was impossible to hike through it.

On this particular day, however, it wouldn't be so bad. It was still early in the season, and the only snow in the woods was from the storm we had on Friday night.

We hiked along Great Bear Heart Mail Route Road, talking about our new snow shoveling business.

"That was a great idea, Shane," I said.

"What was?" Shane replied.

"Taking those business cards around a couple of weeks ago," I said. "When it snowed, people remembered us."

"How much moola did we make?" Dylan piped.

"We earned one hundred forty dollars yesterday," Holly replied. "My mom is going to take it to the bank tomorrow morning. We'll have over four hundred dollars in our account!"

We all slapped gloves, giving one another high-fives. We earned a lot of money with our haunted schoolhouse, and we hadn't spent any of it. Not yet, anyway.

We walked until we came to where the power lines crossed Great Bear Heart Mail Route Road. In the summer, there is a trail that winds along beneath the lines. In the winter, however, the trail is blanketed by snow. For us, that didn't create a problem. We'd been back to Devil's Ridge so many times that we could find it in the middle of the night.

But there *was* an entirely different problem.

Footprints in the snow, along with sled marks.

"Hey," Dylan said, scratching his head. "Somebody else is sledding today."

Which wasn't a problem. The problem was there were three sets of footprints in the new snow . . . and we were pretty sure who they belonged to.

Gary, Larry, and Terry Martin.

We followed the tracks. All around us, on both sides of the power lines, many trees were blackened and burned . . . a reminder of the terrible forest fire from earlier in the summer. I still get a chill when I think about it. We had been caught in the middle of the fire . . . but quick thinking and hard work had saved our lives.

Sure enough, after trudging along the power lines and cutting back into the forest to Devil's Ridge, we could hear the Martin brothers yelling at one another. When we emerged from the forest and stood at the base of the hill, we could see them, standing at the top of Devil's Ridge. Gary had just pushed Larry into the snow. Terry was climbing onto his sled.

"Knock it off!" Larry shrieked, and his voice echoed down the hill.

"Typical Martin behavior," Tony said, shaking his head. "What a bunch of clowns."

Larry saw us and pointed. Terry, who was now careening down the hill on his sled, saw us at the same time.

"I hope he wipes out," Holly snarled.

He didn't, and his sled stopped only a few feet from where we were standing.

"Sorry," Terry said, "we got here first. Go find yourself another hill."

"Get lost," Shane said. "You don't own this land."

"So what?" Terry sneered. "We were here first. I don't want to have to look at your ugly faces all day long."

By this time, Gary and Larry were on their sleds, sliding down the hill. They stopped next to Terry and got to their feet.

"Hey, if it ain't the local do-gooders," Gary said. "Going around and shoveling people's driveways."

"Yeah, and it would be a lot easier if you would mind your own business and not shovel snow back into their driveways," Lyle snapped.

"I don't know what you're talking about," Gary said innocently.

"You know exactly what we're talking about," I replied. "We shoveled those driveways, and you guys pushed a bunch of snow back in."

"So, what if we did?" Terry said, taking a step toward us. "What are *you* going to do about it?"

I could already see where this was heading, and I didn't like it.

But I was mad, and so was Shane, Holly, Lyle, Tony, and Dylan. The Martin brothers were always causing trouble, and, all too often, they got away with it.

Terry leaned over and picked up some snow, balling it up in his hands. "Yeah," he said, "what are you freaks going to do about it?"

And with that, he tossed the snowball—not hard, but hard enough—striking Holly on the cheek.

That was the last straw for Tony Gritter. He lunged like an angry gorilla and was on Terry in an instant. The two tumbled, and Tony buried Terry's face in the snow. Then, Larry got into the act, grabbing a handful of snow and rubbing it in Tony's face.

Things had finally gone too far. Trouble had been brewing . . . and it had finally boiled over.

The rest of us got involved. We tackled Gary and Larry, rubbing snow in their faces. All the while, Tony held Terry down, pressing his face down into the cold snow. We were all yelling and shouting. Terry was doing the worst of the screaming, but his voice was muffled because Tony wouldn't let him up.

"Say you're sorry!" Tony ordered. "Say you're sorry!"

Shane was holding Gary down while I rubbed snow in his face. He was spluttering and spitting. The cold snow had melted, and his face was shiny and wet. Holly and Lyle had succeeded in pinning Larry down face-first, and they were washing his face with snow, too. Dylan was busy stuffing snow down the back of Larry's coat.

Finally, Terry gasped something that sounded like 'I'm sorry', and Tony let up. He stood over Terry as he rolled away. His face was wet and red.

Tony pointed. "If you ever do that again," he fumed, "if you *ever* do that again to one of my friends, you are going to be more than sorry."

Terry scrambled away, rolling in the snow to his sled.

Lyle and Holly released their hold on Larry, and Shane and I stood up. Gary got to his feet.

"And you better not mess with any more of our driveways," Shane said angrily. "Or you'll get it again."

"Come on, guys," Gary ordered. "It's starting to smell around here." He was smarting off, but he sounded defeated.

Without another word, the three Martins grabbed their sleds and trudged off through the snow. We could see them whispering to one another, but we couldn't hear what they were saying.

"That'll teach 'em!" Dylan exclaimed.

"Are you all right, Holly?" Lyle asked.

Holly shrugged. "I'm fine. The snowball didn't hurt."

"Yeah," Tony said, "but he shouldn't have thrown it in the first place."

"Maybe they'll leave us alone from now on," Shane said.

"Maybe," I said. But I wasn't so sure.

As it turned out, I had good reason to feel uncertain. Our problems with the Martin brothers were only beginning.

7

We had a blast sledding that day. It was cold, but we were bundled up really well. Plus, we were having so much fun that we wouldn't have noticed, anyway.

It started snowing around mid-day, and we were all hoping that we'd get another storm. That would mean more customers . . . and more money.

But the snow stopped, and we only got a light dusting . . . not enough to make people want to call us and shovel their driveways. In fact, it didn't snow for another two weeks . . . but when it did, we were ready.

Unfortunately, so were the Martin brothers.

It started snowing on Thursday afternoon, after I got

home from school. The weather report called for five or six inches of new snow by morning . . . not enough to cancel school, but enough that we knew we'd have customers calling. We agreed to meet at the market at six the following morning, because we were sure we'd have a few driveways to shovel before school.

It was still dark when I arrived at the market Friday morning, but the snow hadn't stopped. Lyle, Tony, and Holly were already there.

"Man, this is just too early to get up," Tony complained.

"Hey," Lyle said, "so what? At least this way, we can shovel a few driveways and earn some money before we have to go to school."

Dylan was late, as usual . . . but so was Shane, which was strange. He's usually on time.

Soon, we saw Dylan's form coming toward us, carrying his snow shovel. It was six-fifteen.

But Shane hadn't arrived. In fact, it was nearly six-thirty before we finally saw him trudging down the hill. His hat and shoulders were dusted with the newly-fallen snow.

"Sorry I'm late," he said, as he walked up to us.

"Where's your shovel?" Dylan asked him.

I hadn't noticed it until then, but Shane didn't have

his snow shovel.

He shook his head. "No need," he said. "No one has called. I waited and waited, but the phone never rang."

"What?!?!" Tony crowed, spreading his arms wide. "All this snow, and nobody needs their driveway shoveled?"

"Well, think about it," Shane said. "It's still snowing. No one is going to pay us to shovel their driveway if it's still coming down. Then, they'd have to have their drive shoveled all over again."

That made sense.

"So, what now?" Dylan asked.

"We go to school, just like usual," Shane said.

Tony shook his head. "I could've slept in!" he growled.

"Now you've got more time to do your homework," Holly chirped.

"Yeah, right," Tony said, rolling his eyes.

The snow stopped around lunchtime. We knew that we'd have customers after school let out, so we agreed to go straight home, change, and meet at the market with our shovels.

After school, Holly and I arrived first, followed by Tony, then Shane. He had a confused look on his face.

"We still don't have any customers," he said, shaking

his head. "Mom says the phone hasn't rang all day."

That *was* strange. There was at least six inches of new snow that had fallen since last night . . . enough that people would need their driveways and sidewalks shoveled.

But we didn't get a single call.

"Maybe they're mad at us from the last time," Dylan said. "You know . . . maybe they think that we were the ones who pushed the snow back into their driveways."

Lyle Haywood shook his head. "No," he said. "That's not it. I think everybody thought we did a good job. Most of them said they would call us again."

"Let's walk around," I suggested. "We can knock on doors and try to get some business that way."

"Good idea," Shane said.

We headed out, walking along Great Bear Heart Mail Route Road to some of the places we'd shoveled before.

"Hey," Lyle said. He stopped walking and pointed. "Didn't we shovel that driveway a couple of weeks ago?"

"Yeah," Holly said. "That lady said we did a good job, and she would call us again."

"But her driveway is already shoveled," Dylan said.

I nodded. "Yeah, and whoever did it, didn't do a very good job."

It was true. Whoever had shoveled the driveway left

big piles of snow all over the place. The sidewalk wasn't shoveled at all, and there was no rock salt spread out.

"Let's go ask her," Shane said. "Maybe she did it herself to save money."

We walked up to the house and rang the doorbell. After a moment, the woman answered.

"Hello, Ma'am," Shane said. "We were the ones who shoveled your driveway a couple of weeks ago."

"Yes?" she said.

Tony spoke. "We were wondering why you didn't call us to shovel your driveway. Did we do something to make you mad?"

The woman shook her head. "No," she said. "But a couple of other boys came by a few days ago. They said that they would do the same job cheaper than anyone else . . . so I called them today."

I couldn't believe it! Someone else in Great Bear Heart had started their own snow shoveling business!

"Was it *three* boys?" Holly asked. "A little older than us?"

The woman nodded. "That's right," she said. "They came by today and shoveled the driveway. I'm sorry, but I've got to save money where I can, so I called them first."

"We understand," Shane said. "Thank you."

"Have a nice day," the woman replied. She closed the door, leaving us fuming on the porch.

"Those buggers!" Dylan raged. "They stole our customer!"

"Yeah," Holly exclaimed. "That's not fair!"

We walked down the driveway and back to the street.

"Let's go check some of our other customers," Shane said.

We walked a short way to another driveway, one that we had shoveled after the previous storm. Sure enough, it had been shoveled . . . but not very well.

"We're going to lose all of our customers!" Lyle said. "The Martin brothers are going around and shoveling our driveways!"

"And for less money, too!" Tony spat. "They can't do that!"

"Oh, yes they can," Shane said. "It's called 'competition'. We don't have to like it, but that's just the way things are."

"But Shane," Holly said, "if they take all of our customers, we won't be able to earn any money."

"Let's lower our price!" Tony said. "That'll teach 'em!"

Shane shook his head. "If we lower our price, people will think that the value of our snow shoveling service is less than what the Martins are charging. We do a better job than they do, at a fair price. We have to stick to it. Come on." He started up the driveway.

"Where are we going?" I asked.

"We're going to talk to the owners of this house," he replied. "I'm going to show them something."

Tony shook his head. "Here we go again," he muttered, and the five of us started out after Shane. We had no idea what was up his sleeve . . . but we were about to find out.

Shane marched right up to the front door and rang the doorbell. We stood behind him, waiting.

"What are you going to say?" Dylan whispered.

"Just let me do the talking," Shane whispered back.

The door opened, and a man appeared.

"Yes?" he said.

"Hi," Shane said. "I'm Shane Mitchell, and we shoveled your driveway after the first snowfall of the year."

"Yes?" the man repeated.

"Well, we were just wondering if we did something wrong. We thought you were happy with our job, and were hoping that you'd call again."

"Well," the man said, glancing at each of us, "those three other fellas came by last night, and told me they'd do the same job as you for only six dollars."

"Six dollars?!?!" Dylan hissed.

"Shhhh!" Holly hissed back.

Shane got a real thoughtful expression on his face. "Well, I can see where you want to save money. But do you really think you got your six dollars' worth?"

"What do you mean?" the man asked.

Shane turned around, motioning with one hand. "Step aside, guys."

We shuffled to the side of the porch.

"As you can see," Shane continued, "there is snow piled up in clumps at the edges of your driveway. They didn't actually clear your driveway . . . they just pushed it to the side, because it was easier for them."

The man stroked his chin. "Hmmm," was all he said.

"Notice your walkway?" Shane said, pointing. "It's not shoveled *at all.* They didn't even touch it. We shoveled it spotless when we did it for you."

The man frowned. He looked like he was getting angry.

But Shane wasn't through.

"Lastly, if you look at your drive, it's still very

slippery. When we were here, we put down rock salt so you wouldn't slip and fall. Your driveway, as it is now, is very slick. I'd be careful, if I were you."

"Looks like they didn't do the job they said they would," the man said.

Shane shook his head. "No, they didn't. But we will." He reached into his coat pocket and pulled out a business card. "Call us if we can help."

"I will," the man said. "But I'm going to call those other boys, first."

Dylan gasped. "But . . . but why?!?!" he blurted.

"Because they're going to come back here and do the job they promised," the man said angrily. "As for you six, I want you to shovel my driveway for the rest of the winter."

Our spirits soared.

"You won't be sorry, sir!" Shane exclaimed.

"Yeah!" Tony piped up. "We'll work hard, every time!"

"We're the hardest working kids in the snow business!" Dylan chortled.

"Yes, you are," the man said. "Now, if you'll excuse me, I have an important phone call to make."

With that, the man closed the door, leaving the six of us standing on his porch.

"Shane, that was brilliant!" Holly said.

"Yeah!" Lyle agreed. "You showed him!"

Shane shook his head. "All I did was show him the truth. And the truth is, the Martins tried to cheat him. They told him they would do the same job we did, but for less money. Well, they didn't do what they said they would do, and that's not right."

"But they got caught," I said.

"Let's go show our other customers!" Tony said.

"No," Shane shook his head. He grinned. "I want to hang out here for a while. I'd like to be here when the Martins come back."

Dylan rubbed his gloves together. "Let's ambush them!" he said. "We'll cream them with snowballs when they get here!"

Again, Shane shook his head. He smiled. "We won't have to," he said. "If they do what I think they'll do, they'll wind up ambushing themselves. Come on. Let's hide."

Things were about to get really interesting.

9

We hustled to the side of the garage, waded through the snow, and hid behind some bushes. The leaves were gone, but the branches were thick. We laid down in the snow and had a pretty clear view of the driveway.

Ten minutes later, we heard bickering coming from down the street.

"Here they come!" Shane whispered.

Soon, the Martin brothers were at the end of the driveway . . . and they didn't sound happy. They started shoveling, throwing snow over their shoulders.

"This is too much work!" Gary said angrily.

"Yeah, well, you got us into this!" Larry said.

"Yeah," said Terry. "First, this old man called us. Then, all of our other customers called us! We've got to re-shovel everyone's driveway!"

I almost laughed out loud! Our other customers realized what a shoddy job the Martins had done! They must have called and complained, and insisted they come back and do the job right!

"You said this was going to be easy," Larry said, flinging a shovel full of snow over his shoulder. "Well, this isn't easy! This is hard!"

"Oh, hush up, you sissy!" Gary shot back.

"We're going to be shoveling until midnight!" Terry grumbled. He picked up a shovel full of snow.

"Big deal," Gary said. "We still got paid."

Right then, something inside of Terry just snapped. He was holding his shovel full of snow, and he threw it—right at Gary! A plume of white powder hit Gary in the face, covering his hat, his shoulders . . . everything!

"Oh, you think you're funny, huh?" Gary shouted angrily. He dropped his shovel and lunged at Terry. The two fell into the snowbank.

Larry leapt into action. Now all three of them were wrestling in the snow, grunting and shouting.

"Take that!"

"Knock it off!"

"Oof!"

"Ouch!"

"Hey!"

Not far away, the six of us were hunkered down in the snow, holding our gloves over our mouths to keep from laughing out loud. Seeing the three brothers battling each other was one of the funniest things we'd ever seen.

Finally, after about ten minutes, the Martins finished fighting. They got up, all snow-covered and worn out, picked up their shovels, and continued working without speaking to one another. When they finished, they threw their shovels over their shoulders and headed out to their next driveway. It was going to be a long night for Gary, Larry, and Terry Martin.

Later, at the Great Bear Heart Market, we stood outside and sipped hot chocolate, talking. The temperature had dropped, and it was really cold.

"Serves the Martins right," Holly said. "They tried to steal our customers."

"Well, that might happen again," Shane said. "Other kids might see what we're doing, and start their own snow shoveling business. We just have to make sure that we do good work, all the time."

The next time it snowed, Shane's phone rang off the hook. We were back in business . . . and this time, we no longer had to worry about the Martin brothers. They found out pretty quickly that shoveling driveways was hard work . . . and they wanted no part of that.

We kept a close eye on the weather reports, because we wanted to be sure we were always ready. After all, we had customers who counted on us, and we didn't want to let them down. I got used to Shane's early morning phone calls.

But one morning the phone rang, and it wasn't Shane. It was Dylan Bunker.

"I've got it!" he exclaimed.

"You've got what?" I said groggily.

"I've got an idea for an ice boat, and it won't even cost us a lot of money!"

Which is how we got involved in one of the wildest adventures we ever had.

THE INCREDIBLE ICE BOAT

1

Dylan's idea was pretty simple . . . sort of. He thought that his big sled could be made into an ice boat. All we would need was a mast and a sail.

"You know, that's not a bad idea," Lyle said, as he sipped his hot chocolate. It was Saturday morning, and we were gathered at the Great Bear Heart Market. An inch of snow had fallen overnight, but not enough for anyone to call to have us shovel their driveway. The sky was now a rich, china blue, cloudless.

"But where do we get a mast and a sail?" Tony asked. "Old Man Franklin might have something like that in his junkyard, but he's closed until spring."

"We could use just about anything," Shane said, "as long as it's straight and strong."

"It would need to be about seven feet long," Lyle said, "because the sail would have to be big enough to catch a lot of wind."

"We need something like a big, fat, fishing pole," Dylan suggested, "only a lot stronger."

"Hey," Holly wondered aloud. "How about a clothesline post?"

"A what?" I asked.

"A clothesline post," she replied. "In our back yard, we have a clothesline. It's held up by a post on either end. In the summer, Mom hangs clothes out to dry. But in the winter, she doesn't use it at all. Each post has a crossbar near the top."

"How long are the posts?" Shane asked.

"I'm not sure," Holly said. "But they're about two inches around, and they're made of hard plastic."

"Probably PVC pipe," Tony said.

"What's that?" Dylan asked.

"It's just a hard type of plastic," Lyle replied. "It's used mostly for plumbing. You know . . . drains and stuff like that."

"Oh," Dylan said.

"Would your mom let us use one?" Shane asked.

Holly shrugged. "I don't see why not," she replied. "As long as we don't break it, and we put it back when we're done. All we would have to do is untie the clothesline and pull one of the posts out of the ground."

"And what about a sail?" I asked.

"We could make one out of an old sheet," Lyle suggested. "We could probably find one at the thrift store."

"Everyone in favor of making our own ice boat with Dylan's sled, raise your hand," Shane said.

We raised our gloved hands in the air.

"Settled," Shane said. "Let's go over to Holly's and get one of those poles."

"Yeah!" Tony said. He slapped Dylan on the back. "This is a cool idea!"

"It's going to be a blast!" Dylan hooted. "I want to go super-fast!"

Oh, Dylan was going to get his wish, all right. In fact, he'd be going a lot faster than he could have possibly imagined.

2

When we reached Holly's house, she went inside to ask her mom if we could use one of the clothesline posts. She returned a moment later.

"Mom says that it's fine, as long as we don't break it. And we have to put it back when we're done."

That didn't seem like a problem.

What was a problem, however, was the fact that the poles were frozen in the ground. I guess we figured that we would just pull one of them out, but that's not what happened.

"Let's all try it," Shane said, and the six of us huddled close, each trying to grasp the plastic. It was difficult, because our gloves wouldn't allow for a good grip.

"Hey," Shane said, after several unsuccessful tries. "Let's try heating up the ground with hot water. That might melt the ice and loosen the pole."

"That might work," Lyle said, "but we'll have to be quick. Otherwise, the water will freeze, and we'll be right back where we started."

Holly rushed inside, hustling back a few minutes later with a bucket filled with hot water. She poured it around the base of the pole. The snow surrounding the pole quickly melted away.

"Okay," Shane said. "Now let's give 'er a try."

It worked! It took a few seconds, but the hot water thawed the ground just enough for us to yank the pole from the snow-covered, frozen ground.

"We got it!" Dylan exclaimed.

"This'll work great!" Lyle said, inspecting the pole. "It's really light and strong!"

Shane, Tony, and Lyle took the clothesline post to Shane's house, where they had a heated garage. Dylan ran home and pulled his sled over to Shane's. Then he met up with us at Holly's house, and the three of us hiked to the thrift store.

"We forgot to take money out of the bank!" Dylan suddenly exclaimed, as we plodded through the snow.

"We won't be able to buy any sheets!"

"That's okay," Holly replied. "I have some money. The Club can pay me back."

"I have some money, too," I said. "Only a couple of dollars, though."

As it turned out, we didn't need any money at all. When we told the lady at the thrift store what we wanted the sheets for, she had an even better idea.

"I have an old sheet that someone donated," she said. "It has a couple of rips, and nobody wants it. I was going to throw it away, but if you want it, you can have it."

When she showed us the sheet, we knew we were in business. It was perfect! Sure, it had a few rips, but Holly said she could sew them up without any problem.

Best of all, it was free.

The lady folded the sheet and handed it to Holly. We thanked her, and left.

"This is going to be so cool!" Dylan piped as we trudged on, heading for Holly's house.

"It's going to be a blast, that's for sure!" I agreed. "I can't wait!"

It didn't take Holly long to fix the rips in the sheet. The sail wasn't pretty to look at, but we didn't care. As long as it did the job, we were happy.

When Holly was finished, she stood.

"Help me fold it," she said, "and we'll take it over to Shane's."

After folding the sheet, we scrambled into our coats, boots, and hats, and hurried to Shane's house. He, Tony, and Lyle were in the garage. Dylan's sled was on its side, and the mast protruded from the front of it.

"Just in time," Lyle said, as I closed the garage door behind us. "We're almost finished."

"Our sail is cool!" Dylan whooped, and we explained how we'd gotten the sheet for free, and how Holly had repaired the rips.

"We had a hard time fastening the mast to the sled," Tony explained. "But Mr. Wizard, here, came up with a genius of an idea." He pointed to Lyle.

"Actually, it's pretty simple," Lyle explained. He was holding a wrench, working on the sled. "I drilled some holes near the bottom of the plastic clothesline pole, and we bolted it to the underside of the sled."

"You drilled holes in my mom's clothesline pole?!?!" Holly cried.

"Hey, relax," Lyle assured her. He pointed to where the pole was fastened to the sled. "The holes are near the bottom. When we put it back into the ground, no one will ever know. Did you bring the sail?"

Holly nodded. She unfolded the sheet, displaying her handiwork.

"Perfect!" Shane said.

"But how are we going to connect the sail to the mast?" I asked.

"We already thought of that," Tony said. "Tell 'em, Lyle."

Lyle pointed to the top of the mast. "See how the mast has that bar? It's kind of in the shape of a 'T'. Well, all we have to do is tie one corner of the sheet to each end of the bar. We'll tie a rope to the other two corners of the sheet."

"But that doesn't look anything like a sail," Dylan said. "How is that going to work?"

"I know it won't look like much of a sail," Lyle said, "but its purpose is to catch wind. By tying the two corners to the cross bar and the other two corners to a rope, it will fill out when the wind blows. Hopefully, it will catch enough wind to propel the entire sled—and its rider—across the ice."

"Oh," Dylan said.

"Bring me the sheet, Holly," Lyle ordered. Holly did, and, in no time at all, the sail was connected to the mast. Shane used a thick rope to knot the two opposite corners of the sheet.

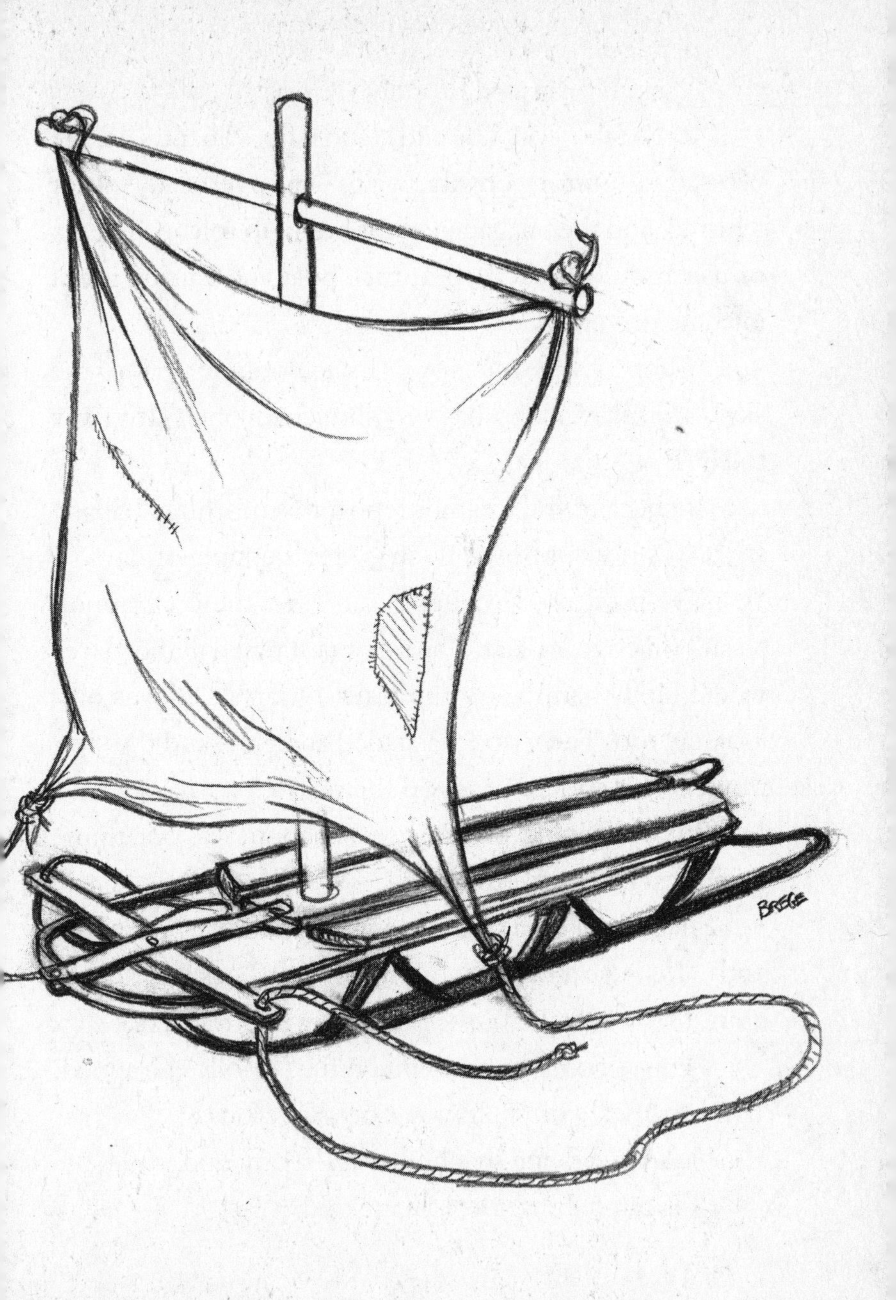
BREGE

"There!" Lyle said proudly. "Good to go!"

"Let's take it outside and stand it up," Shane said. He pressed a button on the wall. An overhead motor whirred, and the big garage door began to roll up. The six of us carefully picked up our ice boat and carried it out into the driveway.

"I hope it doesn't snow," I said, looking up into the sky. "I don't want to have to shovel anyone's driveway today."

"I checked the weather report this morning," Shane said. "It's not supposed to snow for a couple of days."

We stood the sled up. I must say: the contraption wasn't much to look at. The sail was stitched in the places where Holly had to sew the tears. Dylan's sled was old-looking, too. The wood was faded and gray, and the steel runners had spots of rust on them.

But we didn't care. All we cared about was one thing: going fast on Puckett Lake.

Shane looked at his watch. "It's almost noon," he said. "Let's go grab some lunch. Meet back here in an hour, and we'll take our ice boat down to the lake."

"This is going to be so much fun!" Holly exclaimed. "And the best part is, it won't be dangerous."

"Like our flying machine was," Tony said.

"Or our submarine," Shane said.

I shuddered. Our club had built a flying machine we dubbed the *Falcon.* Lyle and Holly had barely escaped with their lives. That same summer, we restored an old research submarine . . . which led to a disaster in Puckett Lake. All six of us could have drowned.

But our ice boat was different. Our ice boat wouldn't leave the ground. And the ice on Puckett Lake was really thick, so we didn't have to worry about breaking through.

No, nothing could go wrong with our ice boat.

At least, at the time, that's what I thought.

But sometimes, no matter how hard you plan, mistakes can still be made. Sometimes, problems arise that you never even thought about beforehand.

And that's what was about to happen.

3

After lunch, Holly picked me up with her dad's snowmobile. This was the first winter that her parents allowed her to drive it by herself, and she was pretty excited. She had an extra helmet in her lap, and she handed it to me. I hopped on the seat behind her, put the helmet on, and we rode to Shane's house.

Shane's family also had a couple of snowmobiles, and our plan was to tie a rope to one of them and pull our ice boat down to the lake. Thankfully, the lake was only a few blocks away, and we didn't have far to take it. Shane and Tony rode one snowmobile, slowly pulling the ice boat. Holly and I rode the other snowmobile, while

Dylan and Lyle walked behind Shane and Tony, keeping the ice boat steady.

There was a strong wind blowing, whipping up snow and sweeping it across the lake. Far out, toward the middle, were several dozen ice shanties. Puckett Lake is a popular ice fishing spot, and there are shanties on the ice all season long. Most shanties aren't very big. They're made out of wood, and they look like tall black boxes seated on the ice. Lyle and his dad have a shanty, and it even has a heater in it. Lyle says that the inside of the shanty gets so warm that he and his dad take their coats off and fish in their T-shirts, even though it's freezing outside.

When Shane pulled our ice boat onto the lake, the wind immediately filled the sail, billowing it out like a white ghost. In the flick of an instant the ice boat was on its side, blown over by the strong gust of wind.

Shane stopped the snowmobile and leapt off. Holly stopped her machine and shut off the engine.

"We're going to have to be careful," Shane said. "It's pretty gusty out here. Let's get 'er back up."

Holly and I grabbed the mast and lifted. Tony grabbed a rope that was tied to the sail, and we were able to get the craft righted quickly. The wind filled the sail again, but Tony let go of the line. The sail flapped like a flag in the stiff, cold breeze.

"Dylan, it was your idea and your sled," Shane said. "Do you want to go first?"

Dylan shook his head. "I've never done anything like this before," he said. "I don't want to go first."

"I'll go," Lyle said. "I've sailed my brother's small sailboat. This can't be much different."

Lyle sat down on the sled, placing his feet on the wood steering bar. Tony handed him the line. When he was ready, he would pull the sail in, catching wind. He would have to hold onto the rope with one hand, and hold onto the sled with the other. He would steer with his feet on the wood handlebar.

"Good luck," Tony said. "Don't crash."

"Piece of cake," Lyle said, and he pulled the rope, drawing the sheet in. Instantly, the sail billowed, and Lyle pulled it in more.

The sled began to creep forward on its steel runners.

"It's working!" Dylan exclaimed. He jumped up and down on the ice. "It is! It's really working!"

The ice boat moved faster.

"Way to go, Lyle!" I shouted.

"Faster!" Shane shouted. "Let's see how fast you can go!"

The ice boat was still picking up speed. Because the

surface of the ice wasn't really smooth, the craft bumped and rocked.

"He's really moving!" Tony said.

"Look at him go!" Holly exclaimed.

Lyle was now only a speck in the distance, but we could see that he was moving very fast. Then, the craft began to turn.

"He's coming back around," Shane said. "Man . . . I can't wait to try it!"

The ice boat was making a long, wide turn. It was a good thing that Lyle had sailed before, because he sure knew what he was doing.

Suddenly, without warning, disaster struck. In the blink of an eye, a gust of wind grabbed the sail, flipping the entire contraption on its side.

Oh, no! Lyle had crashed!

4

Lyle was too far away for us to know if he was hurt or not. All we knew was that there was no movement coming from the crashed ice boat. It looked like a tiny crumple far out into the lake.

"Quick!" Shane said, leaping onto his snowmobile. *"Let's get out there!"*

Tony jumped on the seat behind Shane, and the machine roared to life and quickly sped away. Holly was already on her snowmobile, and I climbed on behind her. Dylan scooted on behind me. "I don't have a helmet!" he shrieked.

"Hang on!" Holly said, and the machine took off,

almost jerking Dylan and me off the back. Soon, we were going a bajillion miles an hour, racing to Lyle's rescue.

As we approached the crash scene, we still couldn't see any movement. I started to get even *more* worried.

Is Lyle all right? I thought. *Is he hurt? Will he have to go to the hospital?*

I tried to think positive, but I was still really worried and anxious.

Shane and Tony arrived ahead of us, stopping only a few feet from the upended ice boat. Tony leapt from the machine.

Moments later, Holly was slowing her snowmobile. We pulled up next to the ice boat. Lyle was on the ground, sitting in the snow. He was rubbing his head. Shane and Tony were working to get the sled righted. Thankfully, both Lyle and the ice boat appeared to be okay.

"Man," Lyle said. "I should've had a helmet. I almost busted my noggin!"

"What happened?" I asked.

"I was trying to turn," Lyle explained. "A gust of wind caught the sail, and I couldn't let it out in time. It tipped over, and I slammed into the ice."

"Ouch," Holly winced.

"Are you all right?" Dylan asked.

Lyle nodded. "Yeah, I'm fine. But I think we ought to wear a snowmobile helmet when we ride this thing. Otherwise, someone's going to really get hurt."

"Good idea," I said.

Shane spoke. "Tony, you come with me. We'll go get two more helmets, so we'll all have one. You guys stay here, and we'll be right back."

Shane and Tony raced off on the snowmobile. In minutes, they returned. Tony was carrying two snowmobile helmets in his arms. Tony handed a helmet to Dylan, and one to Lyle. They slipped the helmets over their heads and fastened them on.

"I'll go next," Shane said. "Tony, you can drive my machine. I'll ride the ice boat back to the park, and someone else can give it a try."

Shane sat on the sled and positioned his boots on the steering bar. Then he picked up the rope that was tied to the bottom two corners of the sheet.

"Wish me luck," he said.

"Don't crack up like I did," Lyle warned.

"This is gonna be fun!" Shane shouted, and he pulled in the sail. Immediately, it billowed out fully, catching wind, sending the sled careening across the ice like a gazelle. I couldn't believe how fast it was going!

"Come on!" Holly exclaimed. "He's going to beat us

to the park!"

Holly and I jumped onto her waiting snowmobile. Dylan climbed on behind me, and we took off. Tony and Lyle were behind us. We sped past Shane, and man . . . he was *flying!* He was holding the sled with one hand, and the rope in the other. The sail was full, and the wind was rocketing the craft across the ice.

We reached the park ahead of Shane, but not by much. Holly slowed the snowmobile and stopped where the ice met the shore. Behind us, Shane was letting out the sail and dumping the wind, which slowed the sled. It stopped a few feet away.

"That was awesome!" Shane exclaimed.

"My turn!" Holly said, leaping from the snowmobile.

We had a ton of fun the rest of the afternoon. When I finally took my turn, I was so excited I could hardly stand it! The craft was hard to get used to at first, because I'd never been sailing before. But I got the hang of it quickly. Soon, I was tearing across the lake, bouncing and bumping. Twice, I nearly wiped out! It was better than any carnival ride I'd ever been on.

Finally, after a few hours of racing around Puckett Lake, we called it quits. We were all tired. Oh, for sure, none of us really wanted to quit. But we were hungry, and it was almost time for dinner, anyway.

"Let's go again tomorrow," Shane suggested, as we stood in front of his garage. We had just dragged the ice boat up from the park and pushed it next to the garage. Lyle took the sail down so it wouldn't flap back and forth in the wind all night.

"Yeah," Tony said. "Let's take 'er out again tomorrow."

"All in favor?" Shane continued.

We raised our hands.

"Motion passed six to zero," he said. "Let's meet at my house at noon. And get ready for another day of fast fun!"

Oh, you can bet I was ready. That was one of the reasons that our club was so cool. We did a lot of really fun things that a lot of other kids think of doing, but never do. I liked building things and trying them out. It was a lot of fun. Besides . . . there wasn't much to do around Great Bear Heart, anyway, and I couldn't see myself sitting inside all day playing video games or watching television. Not when we could build flying machines and ice boats.

And Sunday—the next day—would be another day of fun.

Until something happened on Puckett Lake.

That's when Sunday became one of the worst days in

the history of the Adventure Club.

5

I was awakened Sunday morning by a howling wind that seemed to shake the entire house. It whipped around my bedroom window, pushing against the walls, wailing through the leafless oak and maple trees in our yard. I got up and looked outside. It wasn't snowing much, but man . . . the wind was really screaming. It was a lot windier than it had been on Saturday. When we met at Shane Mitchell's house at noon, the wind was still gusting.

"We're going to go like a rocket!" Tony Gritter said, as he put on his snowmobile helmet. We were all dressed extra-warm. With the wind blowing the way it was, it would be really easy to get cold . . . especially out on the ice, where there were no houses or trees to shelter us from the heavy gale.

Like the day before, Shane and Tony rode a snowmobile and towed the ice boat. Holly rode hers, with me on the back. Lyle and Dylan walked behind the sled. We decided not to rig up the sail until we reached the lake, so we wouldn't have to deal with the wind whipping the craft around. Lyle carried the folded sheet as he walked.

We rode slowly down to the market and crossed the highway. The wind had blown all of the snow from the trees that lined the road. Out on the lake, it looked like a white dust storm. The wind was picking up snow and blowing it across the ice. We couldn't even see the other side of the lake.

"We are going to really fly today!" Holly said loudly over the snowmobile engine.

"Yeah," I replied. "We're going to go ninety miles an hour, I bet!"

We parked at the edge of the frozen lake. I could hear other snowmobiles on the ice, but I couldn't see them through the blowing snow.

Lyle unfolded the sail. It took all six of us to rig it to the mast, because the wind kept whipping it around, back and forth. Dylan had to hold the line that we used to pull in the sail, but the wind kept pulling it out of his gloves. He had to tie it to his wrist to keep it from slipping from his grasp.

Finally, the sail was rigged. The ice boat was ready.

"Who's going first?" I asked.

"I am!" Tony proclaimed. "Hand me the rope, Dylan!"

Dylan was struggling to get the rope untied from his wrist, and he wasn't having much luck. The wind was whipping at the sail, which, in turn, was pulling at the rope, making it impossible to untie.

A sudden, brutal gust of wind snared the sail . . . and the unthinkable happened.

The strength of the wind was too much for Dylan. The rope, still tied to his wrist, jerked him off his feet. He fell to the ice . . . and the ice boat took off like a missile!

"Aaahhhh!" Dylan shouted, as the craft pulled him across the ice.

"Oh, no!" Holly shrieked. "Dylan can't get loose! The rope is still tied to his wrist!"

"Aaa-aaa-aaa-aaa-hhh-hhh-hhh!" Dylan screamed. His shout was broken up because he was bouncing so much on the ice. And the craft didn't tip over, either. With Dylan on the ice and still tethered to the sail, it was enough weight to keep the sled on its runners. Dylan's

body was acting as ballast, balancing the ice boat as it sped away.

Now, you have to remember: it wasn't just *windy.* It was really, *really* windy. A lot windier than it was the day before. In seconds, the ice boat was dragging Dylan across the lake like a mad dragster. Already, it was difficult to see him and the craft in the thick curtain of blowing snow.

"We've got to do something!" Lyle shouted.

"The snowmobiles!" Shane said, racing to his machine. Tony leapt onto the snowmobile seat behind Shane. Holly jumped onto her snow machine and I climbed on behind her.

"Wait for me!" Lyle shouted, and he jumped onto the seat behind me.

I looked through the blinding snow. Dylan and the ice boat had vanished in the thick wall of white.

"Go! Go! Go!" I shouted, as Holly's snowmobile roared. She took off so quickly that I had to grab her to keep from falling off. Lyle had to do the same, only he wrapped his arms tightly around my waist.

"Sorry!" Holly shouted, as the machine snapped forward.

"Just find Dylan!" I shouted back.

Shane and Tony were ahead of us, their dark shapes

blurred by the slashing snow. The taillight glowed faintly, like a tiny red eye.

Still, there was no sign of Dylan.

"Do you see him anywhere?!?!" Lyle shouted from behind me.

"No!" I shouted back.

Suddenly, I caught a glimpse of him up ahead. The ice boat was still racing across the lake, dragging Dylan helplessly behind it. In the next instant, Dylan and the ice boat vanished again in the cloud of blowing snow.

"Faster, Holly, faster!" I shouted, but Holly had already cranked the throttle. We caught up to Shane and Tony, and, to our great relief, we could see Dylan and the sled in the distance. That didn't mean that Dylan was out of danger, by any means. But we could see him, and that was better than not.

"What are we going to do?!?!" I shouted to Holly.

Her helmet shook back and forth. *"I don't know!"* she shouted back. *"The rope is still tied around his wrist!"*

Dylan was still trying to free himself from the line tied around his wrist . . . but he wasn't having much luck. Every time he hit a bump, he lost his grip . . . and he was hitting a *lot* of bumps!

Shane and Tony were riding next to us now, and we were only about thirty feet behind Dylan and the out-of-control ice boat.

"We've got to try to knock the ice boat over!" Shane shouted. "Otherwise, it won't stop until he reaches the other side of the lake!"

I knew what Shane meant. If the ice boat dragged Dylan all the way across the lake, he would wind up crashing into trees, or maybe even someone's house!

Our only hope would be to knock over the ice boat so the wind couldn't fill the sail and continue propelling the craft across the frozen lake.

But how?

Suddenly, Shane sped up, heading off to the left a little bit. Dylan was behind the speeding ice boat, still flailing like a fish out of water.

Shane pulled his snowmobile alongside the ice boat, and Tony looked like he was about ready to jump. It was crazy, I know . . . but Tony was going to try to jump onto the ice boat and use his own body weight to tip it over!

Without warning, Shane's snowmobile hit a bump, and Tony was almost thrown off the back. He sat down on the seat, but only for a moment. After he regained his balance, he stood up again. Shane nudged the machine closer, closer—

Tony leapt!

He landed on the sled, but he didn't have anything to

hold onto. He tried to grasp the mast but missed. Instead, he lost his balance and fell off the side, hitting the ice and rolling like a deranged pencil.

Holly hit the brakes, and our machine lurched to a stop next to Tony. He was covered with snow and completely white.

"Are you okay?" Holly and I asked at the same time.

"I'm fine!" Tony replied.

"Hop on!" Holly ordered.

Now, remember: snowmobiles are made for one or two people. With Lyle behind me, it was already a tight fit. When Tony got on, we were squished! Holly was nearly pressed into the handlebars. I felt like a sardine in a can.

"Everybody hang on!" Holly shouted, but we didn't have to worry. With the four of us on the snowmobile, we weren't going anywhere very fast. The machine was sluggish, and it took a few seconds to get going.

Ahead of us, Shane and his snowmobile were barely visible in the blowing snow. Dylan and the ice boat had vanished, but I knew he couldn't be too far ahead of Shane.

"Doesn't this thing go any faster?!?!" Tony shouted.

"Not with four of us!" Holly shouted back. "We're too heavy!"

It took nearly a full minute, but we finally caught up with Shane. Ahead of him, Dylan was still being pulled along by the wayward ice boat.

"If we don't stop him, he's going to go all the way to the other side of the lake!" Lyle shouted.

I peered over Holly's shoulder . . . and what I saw filled me with horror.

Ice shanties.

Dozens of them, like a little city.

And Dylan and the ice boat were heading right for them!

7

As we drew nearer, even more shanties appeared. There were several dozen of them, each about the size of an outhouse, all of them dark brown or black. It looked like a village of refrigerator boxes.

"He's heading right for them!" Lyle screamed.

Shane sped up to the left side of the ice boat. He tried to nudge it with the snowmobile to knock it over, but it didn't work. The sled twisted sideways, then straightened, still on a collision course with the ice shanty village.

Dylan had given up trying to untie the rope from his wrist and was now just hanging on. He didn't look like he was hurt . . . but he was getting the ride of his life!

"Dylan!" Shane shouted. *"Try and pull yourself up! Pull yourself up the rope and try to climb on the sled!"*

Dylan grasped the rope with his right hand, and pulled. That allowed the line to slack a little, and he used his left hand—the one with the rope tied to it—and reached up, grasping the rope. All the while, the ice boat rocketed across the frozen lake with Dylan in tow, heading straight for the cluster of shanties.

Dylan was making progress, however. If he could pull himself closer to the ice boat, he might be able to climb on the sled . . . or, at the very least, pull the mast over, dumping the wind from the sail and stopping the speeding craft.

But that wasn't going to happen.

A bump suddenly sent Dylan into the air. He lost his grip, and was once again at the mercy of the wildly out-of-control craft, the rope still tied to his wrist.

"Look out!" Holly screamed.

"Dylan!" Shane shouted.

"Oh, no!" I shrieked.

The village of ice shanties loomed directly in front of us. Holly had to turn the snowmobile and slow down, as did Shane.

And for one hopeful second, we thought that Dylan

and the ice boat were going to squeak through, and not hit any of the shanties.

Unfortunately, luck was not on Dylan's side. The sled was completely out of control, and there was nothing we could do as it slammed directly into an ice shanty.

8

When the ice boat slammed into the shanty, it looked like an explosion at the lumber company. Broken pieces of wood went flying. Other things were sent careening through the air, too. I saw a coffee can, some tools, fishing poles, a folding chair, and a radio. Metal crashed and glass broke. A ceramic plate shattered. A broken coffee cup was sent hurtling twenty feet into the air. In less than two seconds, the shanty was completely demolished. Thankfully, there was no one inside it at the time, which was a miracle.

And our ice boat wasn't in much better shape, either. The mast had snapped, and was in two pieces. The sail was in shreds. The steel runners on the sled were bent, and the steering bar was broken.

But if there was any good news, it was the fact that, somehow, Dylan had escaped serious injury. He still had the rope around his wrist, but he had managed to roll to the side at the last moment, and he hadn't hit the shanty or the ice boat.

We leapt off the snowmobile and raced to Dylan, laying on the ice next to the pile of debris. Shane, too, had jumped from his snowmobile and was racing across the ice. A couple of fishermen had heard the noise, and they came out of their shanties to see what was going on.

Dylan rolled over and got to his knees. A few small pieces of wood fell off of him.

"Are you all right?" I asked, as we reached him.

"Yeah," Dylan said in disgust. "That wasn't fun! That wasn't fun *at all!*"

Now that he wasn't being pulled by the sled, it was easy for him to untie the rope from his wrist.

"You sure you're okay?" Shane asked.

"I'm fine," Dylan replied. His coat had a rip in it, but that was all. "I'm glad I had a helmet on, though," he said. "It probably saved me from getting killed!"

"Yeah, that would have really messed up your day," Tony said.

"You kids all right?" a man called out from not far away. We turned to see a man standing in the door of his shanty.

"Yeah, we're fine," Holly shouted back.

The man waved, went back into his shanty, and closed the door.

"Somebody is really going to be mad when they find out their shanty is destroyed," I said.

"We have to find out who it belongs to," Shane said, "and go tell them."

I kind of figured that's what we'd have to do, and I wasn't looking forward to it. After all . . . how do you tell someone that you just destroyed their ice fishing shanty?

"There should be a name on the wood somewhere," Lyle said. "My dad says that you have to have your name on your shanty. He says it's the law."

We found the name easily enough. It was painted on the side of the shanty in big letters. Of course, the wood was in several pieces, so we had to find them and put them together like a puzzle so we could read the name.

"Fred Mullbringer," Shane read out loud. "3595 Sprinkle Road. That's right up the street from my house."

"It's a good thing he wasn't inside his shanty when our ice boat hit," Holly said.

"He's going to be madder than a wet cat when we tell

him we wrecked his shanty," Tony said.

Lyle shrugged and frowned. "Well, there's nothing we can do about it now."

"We're going to be in a lot of trouble," Dylan said, surveying the damage. "I think everything is broken."

"Let's pick up what's left of it and make a pile," I said. "That way, it won't get scattered all over the ice."

"Good idea, Parker," Shane said, and we got to work gathering up what was left of the shanty and its contents. When we had all of the debris in a pile, Shane tied what was left of our ice boat to his snowmobile, and we headed back across the lake. Tony and Lyle rode with Shane, and Dylan and I rode with Holly.

I was dreading having to tell Mr. Mullbringer about his shanty. I didn't know him, but I was sure that he would hit the roof when we told him what we'd done. Worse . . . he might even call the police.

Soon, we were parked at Shane's house.

"Let's get a hot chocolate at the market and think about what we're going to tell him," Dylan suggested.

Shane shook his head. "We already know what we're going to tell him," he said. "Let's just get it over with. Then we'll get hot chocolates."

"If we're still alive," Tony said.

We took off our helmets and sat them on the

snowmobiles. It was still as windy as ever, although here, with trees and houses all around, it wasn't nearly as gusty as it was on the lake.

Wordlessly, we trudged down the street, turned onto Sprinkle Road, and stopped in front of a mailbox.

"3595 Sprinkle Road," Shane said. "This is the place."

There was a car and a truck in the driveway, and lights on in the house.

"Time to swallow the toad," Tony said.

Dylan gasped. He looked horrified. "Toad?!?!" he spluttered. "I'm not swallowing any toad!"

"It's just an expression," Tony explained. "When you have to do something you don't want to do. Besides . . . where are we going to find a toad in *this* weather?"

We walked up the driveway and stepped onto the porch. Shane rang the doorbell. After a moment, we heard a shuffling sound, and muffled footsteps. The front door opened, and a man stood in the doorway, looking at us.

"Yes?" he said.

"Mr. Mullbringer?" Shane asked.

"That's me," the man replied. "What can I do for you?"

"You can let us live," Tony mumbled from behind me.

"Ssshhh!" Holly scolded quietly.

"I'm Shane Mitchell," Shane said.

"I'm Lyle Haywood," Lyle said.

After we'd introduced ourselves, Shane dropped the bomb.

"We demolished your ice shanty," he said.

Mr. Mullbringer said nothing. He just stared.

"It was an accident, honest!" Dylan piped. "We didn't mean to! Our ice boat got out of control!"

Tony spoke. "Dylan, here, almost got killed. He's okay, but your shanty is kaput."

Mr. Mullbringer looked dazed. "You . . . you mean there's nothing left of it?" he asked.

"Not really," Shane said. "Just a bunch of pieces and parts."

"Where do you kids live?" Mr. Mullbringer asked. He looked like he was getting angry.

"In town," I said. "We all live here in Great Bear Heart."

"I'm going to go out and see what you kids did," he said. "And you're going to have to pay for the damage. Meet me back here in an hour."

We walked back into town and went to the market. None of us said a word until we got there. George

Bloomer, the owner, waved to us as we walked inside. He could tell something was wrong.

"What's up, guys?" he said. "You look bummed out."

"That's because we are," I said.

"Yeah," Dylan said. "We're in a lot of trouble."

After we explained what had happened, Mr. Bloomer shook his head. "Well, I'm glad you guys weren't hurt. But it was an accident. Tell you what . . . I'll buy you each a hot chocolate."

"Thanks," Holly said.

"Yeah," Dylan echoed. "That's really nice of you."

The hot chocolate tasted good, but it didn't make us feel much better. We knew that more bad news was on its way . . . just as soon as we returned to Mr. Mullbringer's house.

We hung around outside the market, sipping our hot chocolate and watching the wind blow the trees.

"Hey, it's not so bad," Lyle said. "It could have been a lot worse. Dylan could have really been hurt."

"Lyle's right," Holly said. "It could have been much worse than it was."

Finally, after nearly an hour of sulking at the market, it was time to head back to Mr. Mullbringer's house. Once again, we walked all the way to his house without saying a word. We stood on his porch, and Shane knocked. The door opened, and Mr. Mullbringer appeared. He had a handful of papers in one hand.

And he didn't look happy.

"Yeah, you sure wrecked my shanty," he said. "I've gone through all of the receipts of the things you broke, and I made a list of what each item costs. There were a few things that I could salvage, like a couple of tools and my fishing lures. But you broke all of my ice fishing poles, my chair, my radio, and the shanty itself. To replace everything, you owe me three hundred and fifty dollars."

At first, I thought I heard wrong.

Three hundred and fifty dollars?!?! I thought. I could tell Shane, Holly, Tony, Lyle, and Dylan were thinking the same thing.

"Three . . . three hundred and fifty dollars?" Shane said, stumbling through his words.

"That's right," Mr. Mullbringer replied. He waved the receipts in the air. "You can look it over if you want, and you'll see how it all adds up. The radio itself cost nearly ninety dollars. Now, I don't know where you kids are going to get that kind of money, but—"

"Oh, we'll get the money," Holly said. "We've been shoveling snow all winter. Can we bring it to you tomorrow?"

Mr. Mullbringer nodded and glanced at each of us. "That's fine, I guess," he said.

"Okay, then," Holly said. "We'll see you tomorrow."

We walked away silently, in shock. I thought that we would owe the guy fifty or sixty dollars . . . which is still a lot of money. I never dreamed that the damage would cost three hundred and fifty. Sure, we had that much in our club savings account, but we worked hard for it, shoveling snow all winter. It would take a long time to make up for it . . . if we would be able to at all.

The next day, after school, Holly went to the bank and took out the money. The six of us met at her house and walked back to Mr. Mullbringer's. It was heartbreaking to watch Holly count the money out loud as she handed it to him. He thanked us, and we apologized again.

"Well, we saved a lot of money building our ice boat," Lyle said, as we walked back to town, "but it sure wound up costing us."

"How much do we have left in our club savings?" I asked.

"Sixty-three dollars and eighteen cents," Holly replied glumly. "But don't forget . . . we broke my mom's clothesline post, and we have to replace it. She wasn't mad when I told her what happened, but she said the post is about ten dollars."

"Well, at least we'll have a little money left," Dylan said. "We didn't lose all of it."

"We're going to have to work extra hard to make up for it before winter ends," Lyle said. "We still have a couple of months left."

"Hopefully, we'll get a huge snowstorm soon," Tony said. "Then, we'll have a lot of customers that need their driveway shoveled."

Well, Tony was going to get his wish, all right . . . and soon.

But if you know anything about winter storms in Michigan, you know that they can be fierce . . . and unpredictable. What we thought was going to be a boom for our business was about to become one of the most dangerous situations we'd ever found ourselves in.

BLIZZARD

1

My dad says there's one thing you can count on when it comes to Michigan weather: it's consistently unpredictable. Meaning that it's likely to change at any moment, no matter what the weather forecasters say. One time, the television weatherman said that we weren't going to get any snow that night . . . but when I woke up, we had so much snow that school was cancelled.

For the most part, however, the forecasters are right. So, when a snowstorm started brewing out west, hundreds and hundreds of miles away, all of us in the Adventure Club paid close attention to the weather reports. The storm was slowly headed our way, and we hoped to get oodles and oodles of snow. After all, we had a lot of money to make up for, after our accident with the ice boat and Mr. Mullbringer's ice shanty. Every snowstorm meant that we'd have customers calling to shovel their driveways, porches, and sidewalks . . . which, of course, meant more money for our bank account.

But I got a call from Shane on Friday night.

"Bad news," he said. He sounded downhearted.

"What?" I replied.

"I just heard on the radio that the snowstorm is going to go north of us," he said. "We're not going to get any snow at all."

That *was* bad news. All week long, the weather forecasters had been talking about the big storm that was on its way. They said we were going to get over eight inches of snow . . . which would be great for our snow shoveling business. The storm was supposed to hit Friday night, which would have been perfect. We would have had all weekend to shovel snow and earn money.

Now, however, the storm was going to go to the north . . . meaning that we wouldn't get hardly any snow at all.

"I've already told Tony and Dylan," Shane said. "We figured that we'd build a snow fort tomorrow. We'll meet at my house in the morning."

I hung up. On one hand, I was disappointed, because I'd been looking forward to earning a lot of money this weekend. But we'd been talking about building a snow fort all winter. Now that we didn't have to shovel driveways, we would have all day to work on our fort.

And it wouldn't be just *any* snow fort, either . . . but one that would be big enough for all six of us, like an igloo. Holly sketched a design on paper, complete with measurements and everything. We would use blocks of snow to create a rounded dome with a small doorway and a few air holes. It would be built out in the woods, so other kids wouldn't find it and wreck it . . . meaning, of course, the Martin brothers. If they knew about our snow fort, they would demolish it for sure.

The weather forecasters were right. When I awoke on Saturday morning, there wasn't any new snow on the ground. The sky was gray and overcast, but there was no snow falling. The storm had gone north of us, after all.

We met in front of Shane's house at nine o'clock. The temperature had actually warmed up a little, and was nearing thirty degrees. The snow was wet and packy . . . perfect for making snowballs, snowmen . . . and snow forts.

"This is going to be cool!" Dylan said, as he tossed a snowball back and forth in his gloves. "I mean . . . I really wanted to earn some money shoveling snow . . . but building a fort is going to be a lot more fun!"

"And it won't cost us anything, either," I said.

Holly arrived, pulling her toboggan. Shane had asked her to bring it, saying that we might need it to haul blocks of snow to our fort.

"But how are we going to make the blocks?" Tony asked.

"Lyle already thought of that," Shane said. "Check this out."

We waited as Shane went into his garage. He returned a moment later with three pieces of plywood, each about two feet square.

"We use these," Shane explained. He dropped two of the pieces onto Holly's toboggan, and carried one to the edge of the driveway. Then he walked into his yard where the snow was thick and deep.

"All we do is use a piece of plywood to cut down into the snow," he explained. As we watched, Shane held the edge of the plywood and pressed it into the snow like a knife. When he withdrew it, there was a long, half-inch wide incision. Then he turned the piece of wood and did it again, connecting the slices until it looked like he had made a box in the snow.

"Oh, I get it!" Holly said.

Shane nodded. "Watch." He carefully reinserted the plywood into one of the slits in the snow. When it was all the way down, he angled the piece of wood and pushed it beneath the square he had made. Working it back and forth, he pulled up and back . . . and on top of the plywood was a perfect snow brick.

"That's cool!" I exclaimed.

"Yeah!" Dylan agreed. He spread his arms wide. "We'll be able to build a *huge* snow fort!"

Shane dropped the brick and shook the snow off the plywood.

"With three of these things," he said, holding up the piece of wood, "it should go pretty fast."

"Where are we going to build it?" Holly asked.

"In the forest, behind *Rollers,*" Lyle replied. "We can follow the snowmobile trail into the woods, and hike back in a little ways. It'll be far enough away so that no one will see our fort, but we won't be too far from town."

Rollers was a popular bar and grill, just out of town on the main highway that winds through Great Bear Heart. It has a great view of Puckett Lake, so it's busy all year.

Lyle pulled the toboggan, and we started out. We walked down to the main road, following the shoulder south until we passed *Rollers*. Then we headed west, hiking along the snowmobile trail, following it into the woods. All the while, we talked about our fort.

"I'll bet nobody around here has ever built a snow fort like we're going to," Shane said.

"A real igloo!" I exclaimed. "Just like the Eskimos make!"

"And it'll be big enough for all of us to fit in," Lyle said.

Dylan was walking in front. Every once in a while he would pick up a gob of snow and wad it up into a snowball. Then he'd pick a target—usually a nearby tree—and let the snowball fly. Most of the time, he missed.

Suddenly, Dylan stopped in his tracks. *"Holy smokes!"* he exclaimed. His arm shot out in front of him. *"Wolves!"*

We froze.

Up the trail, running toward us at breakneck speed, were two huge wolves!

2

Now, there's one thing you need to know: there have been rumors about wolves in and around Great Bear Heart for years, but no one has actually *seen* any. We have coyotes around, but they are a lot smaller than wolves. My dad thinks that most people mistake coyotes for wolves. He says there are wolves in Michigan's Upper Peninsula and in other states, but not around Great Bear Heart.

But, at that very moment, two wolves were running right toward us! They were attacking!

And there was no time to get away, either. There was no way we were going to be able to outrun two wolves.

They were *fast.*

Suddenly, we heard a cry from the woods.

"Bert! Ernie! Get back here!"

The wolves slowed to a trot . . . but they were still coming toward us.

"Bert! Ernie!"

"Oh, for goodness sakes," Holly said. "They aren't wolves . . . they're *dogs!"*

"They're huskies," Tony said.

A man and a woman suddenly appeared on the trail, coming toward us. They were cross-country skiing.

The huskies were no longer running. They bobbed up to us, wagging their tails.

"Don't worry," the woman hollered, as she skied toward us. "They're very friendly, and they won't bite."

One of the huskies bounded up to me, and I petted his head. Then he galloped over to Holly, who also petted him.

The two skiers approached us and stopped.

"Sorry about that," the man said. "I hope Bert and Ernie didn't scare you."

"They named their huskies Bert and Ernie?" Tony snickered in my ear. *"How goofy is that?"*

"Usually," the woman explained, "we have them on a leash. But when we ski this far back in the woods, we let them run around. They love the snow."

"We were freaked out for a minute," Dylan said. "We thought they were wolves!"

The man and woman laughed. "Bert and Ernie?!?!" the man exclaimed. He shook his head. "They're husky and shepherd mix. They look vicious, but they wouldn't harm a fly! Come on, guys!"

He whistled, and the two dogs ran to him. "You kids have fun," he said, and the pair skied off down the trail with the big huskies leading the way.

"I can't believe they named their huskies 'Bert' and 'Ernie'," Shane said.

"They should have named them 'Fang' and 'Killer'," Lyle said. "That would be more fitting."

We all had a good laugh. The whole situation was kind of funny.

"Come on," Shane said, stepping off the trail. Immediately, he sank up to his knees in snow. "Let's hike back in a little ways, where no one will be able to see our fort."

The snow was deep, and it was difficult to walk after we left the trail. In some places, it was almost impossible to move.

"We should have snowshoes," Tony grumbled.

"Yeah," Holly agreed. "This is hard."

"We won't go too far," Shane said. "Just far enough so that we can't see the trail."

Finally, we stopped at a small clearing.

"Here we go," Shane said, spreading his arms wide. "This spot will be perfect!"

We got to work. Shane, Tony, and Lyle began making snow bricks. Holly, Dylan, and I began arranging them in a circle. It actually worked out well, because Tony, Shane, and Lyle began in the area that would be inside our finished fort. So, as they made snow bricks, they cleared the space for us. We placed the cubes side-by-side, forming a large circle, leaving one small space open for a doorway. Then, we placed more bricks on top of that row, continuing our way around, careful to arrange them in a way that, with each row, they tilted more and more toward the center, giving the fort a dome-shaped appearance.

Holly's toboggan came in handy, too. We made snow bricks, loaded them onto the sled, and pulled it back to our igloo. It was a lot easier than carrying the cubes one-by-one.

Everything was going great. We were having fun, and the fort was looking really cool. We fashioned a short, tunnel-like door, and the structure really *did* look like a real, honest-to-goodness igloo . . . just like the Eskimos make.

And then we heard shouting in the distance.

Laughter.

Right away, we knew who it was.

Gary, Larry, and Terry.

The Martin brothers.

3

"Everybody duck down!" Shane hissed. *"Hide on the ground, in the snow! We don't want them to find our fort!"*

We dropped into the snow, laying down flat. I could hear the Martin brothers in the distance, laughing and yelling at one another.

"Come on!" I heard Larry say. "Their tracks are going this way!"

Oh, no! They were following our tracks! They would lead the Martins right to us!

I could hear footsteps in the snow, not far away.

"They're this way!" Larry insisted.

"No, they're not!" Gary shouted from farther away.

He sounded like he was still on the snowmobile trail. "I don't see them. They probably just hiked back a ways and came back. Come on!"

The soft crunching of footsteps in the snow stopped, and I knew that Larry wasn't too far away.

What if he sees our fort? I wondered. The Martins were always trying to give us a hard time about everything. If they knew where our fort was, they'd come back when we weren't around and wreck it . . . just to have something to do. We knew they would, which was why we built it so far back in the woods.

Then, I heard the footsteps in the snow again . . . moving away.

He hadn't seen us! Larry hadn't spotted our fort! He was walking away!

"Get a move on, slowpoke!" Terry scolded. "We haven't got all day!"

"I'm coming!" Larry snapped back.

We waited, laying in the snow, until we could no longer hear the Martins. Finally, Shane gave the all-clear, and we scrambled to our feet.

"Those guys are always trying to cause trouble for us," Holly said, brushing snow from her coat and pants.

"And they always will," Tony said. "It's just a fact of life."

"Let's forget about them," Lyle said. "Our fort is almost done. Let's finish it."

We only needed another nine snow bricks to complete our igloo. When the last brick was in place, we stood back to admire our work.

"We've got to get a camera!" Dylan said. "This thing is super-duper cool!"

"Let's go inside," Tony said, dropping to his knees. He crawled through the entry way, and vanished. Dylan was next, followed by Holly, Lyle, me, and then Shane, who placed one of the pieces of plywood over the doorway.

"Wow," Holly said. "It sure is dark in here!"

It was, too. The bricks of snow hardly let in any light at all. Once Shane had covered the entrance with the piece of plywood, all I could see were shadows of my friends. The only light coming through was from four air holes, each about the size of a baseball. It would be important to keep them clear so that we'd have enough air to breathe.

"This is awesome!" Lyle exclaimed. "It's the coolest snow fort in the world!"

We went home for lunch, after agreeing to meet back at our fort afterwards. Dylan was the first to return. When Holly and I arrived, we found him inside the fort, reading a comic book with a flashlight. Shane arrived right after Holly and me. Lyle and Tony showed up about twenty minutes later. Shane put the piece of plywood over the door and sealed us in.

And for the next two hours, we stayed in our fort. We had a great time! All we did was talk and joke. We talked about movies that we'd seen, and ones we'd wanted to see. We talked about books that we'd read. Everybody knew that I was working on writing my own book, but I wouldn't tell them what it was about. Not yet, anyway. Not until I was finished. I just told them that it was about us and the Adventure Club, and I wouldn't say anything more.

But we had a great time. We talked about some of the cool things we'd done, and we planned some really fun adventures for the summer. For sure, we would have some more adventures with our submarine, *The Independence.* We talked about the annual fishing derby that is held in Puckett Lake, and how it would be fun to enter. Lyle was a good fisherman, and we thought we just might have a chance of winning.

Another thing we talked about was a camping expedition in the wilds of Michigan's Upper Peninsula. Oh, there was no way it would ever happen. After all . . . we were just six kids. Our parents would never allow us to do something like that.

But it was fun dreaming and talking about it.

Soon, we'd lost all track of time. We were having so much fun, and we didn't have a care in the world.

Until Holly noticed something.

"Doesn't it seem like it's gotten darker?" she asked.

I looked around. Yes, it *did* appear darker. It was really noticeable through the four ventilation holes.

"It shouldn't be getting dark so early," Lyle said, as he crawled to the entry way. He pushed the piece of plywood away, and a murky, gray light streamed through.

"Wow!" he exclaimed. "It's really snowing outside!"

From where I sat in the igloo, I couldn't see out the small doorway. Neither could anyone else. One by one, we scrambled out of the fort.

And when I crawled out of the igloo on my hands and knees, I couldn't believe what I was seeing.

It wasn't just snowing . . . it was *dumping!* The snowflakes were the size of marshmallows, and there was already four or five inches of new snow!

"Looks like our snow shoveling business is going to keep us busy tomorrow!" Shane exclaimed.

"If this keeps up, we'll have a foot of new snow in no time!" Tony said.

We climbed back into our igloo, and Shane placed

the plywood over the door.

"This is great!" Holly said. "We can stay in our igloo and the weather won't even bother us!"

And that's just what we did. We remained inside and continued talking and laughing and joking around.

Until we heard something.

Lyle had been speaking, talking about building another ice boat. "We can make it like—"

A low howl caused him to stop talking.

"What is that?" Dylan asked.

"I think it's the wind," Holly replied. She crawled over to the door. Another howl, louder and longer, seemed to shake our igloo. The blowing wind sounded like an angry old ghost.

As soon as Holly pushed the plywood away from the entrance, a rush of cold air and snow burst inside. It was so sudden that it surprised Holly, and she hesitated before she climbed out.

"It got cold," Tony said.

"It's freezing!" Lyle said.

We climbed out . . . only to find ourselves in the wildest, fiercest, raging snowstorm we'd ever seen. The temperature felt like it had dropped twenty degrees. The snowflakes were no longer big and fluffy. They were like tiny ice pellets, and the wind drove them so hard that they stung my face. It was snowing and blowing so violently that we could barely make out the trees only a few feet away.

"Man," Shane said loudly. "The storm has gotten a lot worse. We'd better head home."

We started out through the woods, anxiously talking about our snow shoveling business and how much money we would earn. This was easily the biggest snowstorm of the year, and I knew that Shane's phone would be ringing off the hook. As we made our way through the blinding snow, we were excited . . . until Lyle made an observation.

"Shane," he said, covering his face with his gloves to block the whipping wind and snow, "shouldn't we have reached the trail by now?"

"I was just thinking the same thing," Holly said.

"I thought it was right over here," Shane replied. "I mean . . . I *thought* it was. Our tracks from earlier today have already been covered up by snow."

A tickle of fear nagged at me. We stopped and tried to get our bearings.

"I think the highway is over that way," Lyle said. He pointed.

"No," Tony said, pointing in an altogether different direction. "I think we have to head that way."

"How can we be lost?" Dylan asked. "We're not that far from town."

"But it's snowing and blowing so bad that we can't see where we're going," I shouted over the raging wind and searing snow.

"If we head in the wrong direction," Shane replied loudly, "we could be in the woods for a long time."

"I'm getting cold," Holly said.

I was, too. I think we all were.

"We have to go back to our igloo while we can still follow our tracks back," Shane said. He pointed to the snow at his knees. "Look. The snow is already covering them up."

"But *then* what, Shane?" Tony asked.

"We'll just wait it out," Shane said. "It can't go on like this for much longer."

We backtracked through the snow and wriggled into our igloo. Once we were out of the wind and blowing snow, the inside of our fort seemed warm. Shane covered the entrance with the plywood, and we waited, not knowing that the storm had settled over Great Bear Heart and Puckett Lake, not knowing that it wasn't about to let up.

And not knowing that we were no longer in the midst of a snowstorm. No, it was worse—much worse than that. The storm that was supposed to have gone north of us had unexpectedly reversed itself and headed south, settling in right over Great Bear Heart.

We were dead-center in the worst blizzard ever to hit northern Michigan in over one hundred years.

4

The storm became a savage lion.

The snow's icy claws ravaged our igloo from all sides. A harsh wind roared and snarled, and its teeth gnashed and snapped all around us, lashing at the trees and tearing at our fort. It was actually kind of cool, being in our fort, safe from the brute force of the brutal storm.

But that tickle of fear inside of me was growing, and I began to realize that we might be in more trouble than we'd thought.

If this storm doesn't let up soon, we could be stuck here overnight, I thought. *And no one will come looking for us until the weather breaks.*

"Some adventurers we are," Tony muttered. "We don't have any way to start a fire or keep warm."

"And we don't have any food or water," I said.

"Somebody will find us," Dylan said hopefully.

Shane shook his head. "Not until the snow stops," he said. "Nobody will go out in this weather. I bet all of the roads and highways are closed."

Holly picked up the stick she'd been using to clear the air holes. She poked it through the hole nearest her, then handed it to Tony, and he used it to poke open the air hole near him. We had to clear them out every few minutes, because it was snowing so hard that they were getting clogged really fast.

"Can't we do *anything?*" Tony asked.

"Yeah," Lyle said. "We can wait. We can wait until the storm passes."

"But that might be hours," Dylan whimpered. "My parents are going to ground me until I'm sixty."

"If only we'd thought to bring a compass," Lyle said. "Then it wouldn't have mattered if we found our tracks, or the trail."

"Well, we have to make do with what we've got," Shane said.

"Yeah," I replied somberly. "But we don't have anything."

"We have shelter," Shane said. "We might not have food or water, but we can at least stay out of the storm."

"We can eat snow," Dylan said. "It will melt in our mouths."

Lyle shook his head. "Bad idea," he warned. "Eating snow will cool your body temperature down. Didn't you pay attention in science class?"

"You're a year older than me!" Dylan said defiantly. "I don't even know that stuff yet!"

"Is anybody getting cold?" Shane asked.

We shook our heads. Outside, in the gusting wind and snow, we'd all gotten cold quickly. Thankfully, it wasn't so bad in our igloo, and we were able to get warm.

"Shane's right," Holly said. "We have to look on the bright side. Just having our igloo is probably going to save our lives. If we got lost in the blizzard, we would probably freeze to death."

The seriousness of our situation was sinking in. We were six kids, all alone in a raging blizzard. There really was nothing we could do until the storm passed.

"At least the forest isn't on fire," Lyle said, reminding us of the time we got caught in a forest fire. That had been a close call, but we'd made it out okay.

"Yeah," Dylan said, "I guess you're right. All we have to do is wait."

"Anyone have any good jokes?" I asked.

"Yeah," Tony snorted. "Us."

That made us laugh a little. Tony was a born joker, and he was always doing or saying something to get a chuckle.

We tried to keep talking about other things—anything—besides the raging blizzard, which, even after an hour, didn't show any signs of letting up. The wind was the only thing we heard for a long time.

Until Holly heard something else.

"What was that?" she asked.

"What was what?" Shane replied.

"I thought . . . I thought I heard something," Holly said. "Like . . . voices."

We listened for a moment.

Dylan shook his head. "I don't hear anyth—"

And then, we *all* heard it.

Shouting! We could hear voices through the howling wind and snow!

"Someone came looking for us!" Holly exclaimed. "We're rescued! Someone came to get us!"

Boy, was she ever wrong.

5

The shouts grew louder, and we all crawled toward the small entrance at the same time. Lyle was the first to reach it, and he pushed away the piece of plywood. Once again, cold air and snow rushed in . . . but we didn't care. We were rescued! People had been looking for us, and we were saved!

"Over here!" Lyle shouted, as he scrambled out of the igloo. The rest of us followed.

"Here we are!" Shane yelled over the screaming wind. "We're right here!"

Our hopes were dashed when we received an answer.

"Oh, man! We're lost! We need help!" someone

shouted, and, even through the deafening roar of the blizzard, we knew who it was.

Gary Martin.

"What's he doing out here?" Tony asked.

"You've got me," Shane said.

"Help!" Gary yelped. "Somebody!"

"Over here!" Shane shouted.

"Keep yelling!" Larry's voice rose over the wind and snow. "Keep yelling, so we can find you!"

"We're right here!" Shane called out again. "This way! Over here!"

A dark blob appeared through the curtain of blowing snow.

"That's it!" Shane said. "We're right here!"

The dark blob took shape, and we could see the Martin brothers huddled together, trudging through the deep snow. Gary was on the left, and Larry was on the right. Terry was in the middle, and it appeared that his brothers were helping him walk.

"What are you guys doing out here?!?!" Tony shouted.

"We got lost!" Gary replied. He raised one arm to shield his face from the lashing snow. "We got lost in the storm. Terry is really cold! He can't feel his feet or his hands!"

That wasn't good. If Terry was that cold, it meant frostbite was setting in. He needed to get warm—and fast.

"Bring him into our igloo!" Shane ordered. "Let's get out of the wind!"

Tony and I climbed inside first, and we helped Terry get through the entrance. Gary and Larry were next, followed by Dylan, Shane, Holly, and Lyle.

With the nine of us inside it was cramped, and there wasn't much room to move. Terry was on his back, shivering.

"What were you guys doing out in the storm?" Shane asked Gary.

"Looking for you guys," Gary replied. "We knew you were building a fort somewhere. We were trying to find it. When it started snowing hard, we couldn't find our way back through the woods."

I was surprised to hear Gary speaking that way. Usually, he smarts off to us. Now, however, he seemed worried. Worried . . . and *scared.*

"Didn't you try and follow your own tracks?" Lyle asked.

Larry nodded. "For a while, we did. But soon, the snow covered them up. We've been wandering around for a couple of hours."

"We've got to get Terry warm," Holly said urgently. "He's freezing."

"But we can't leave the igloo," I said. "Otherwise, we'll get lost. We'll all freeze."

"I have some matches," Gary said. "I tried to start a fire, but the wind was too strong."

"Funny," Tony spat. "You didn't have a hard time starting a fire last summer." It was a direct reference to last year, when the Martins had been shooting off fireworks in the woods. They started a forest fire that almost burned the town down. Thankfully, fire crews had been able to stop it before it reached Great Bear Heart.

"All right," said Shane. "Here's what we're going to do." He looked at me. "Parker and Dylan . . . you guys go out and get some wood for a fire. Don't go far. Just find some dead branches, brush the snow off them, and bring them back. Gary and Larry . . . you guys help Parker and Dylan. Lyle and Tony . . . you guys help me poke a hole in the roof of our igloo. There's no wind here, so we should be able to get a fire going. The smoke will rise up and out through the hole that we make. Holly . . . stay by the door of the igloo, and take the wood when the guys hand it to you. Build a pile in the middle of the fort."

Dylan and I got to work, along with Gary and Larry Martin. I couldn't believe that we were actually doing something together! The Martin brothers were our sworn enemies!

But, then again, we didn't want anything to happen to Terry. We didn't like them . . . but we didn't want them to get hurt . . . or worse.

Thankfully, we found a lot of dead branches without having to go far from the igloo. We carried them back and pushed them through the entrance, where Holly grabbed them and made a pile in the middle of our fort.

Lyle, Tony, and Shane created a hole in the top of the igloo by removing two blocks of snow. However, there was already ten inches of new snow on top, so it had to be cleared off. Plus, they had to be careful not to knock any other blocks loose. The last thing we needed was to have the whole fort cave in!

Shane shouted from inside the fort. "Okay," he said. "That's enough wood for now."

Dylan, Gary, Larry, and I dropped to our knees and crawled through the entrance.

Shane continued barking orders. "Lyle . . . put the plywood back over the door, but not all the way. We need to keep the wind and snow out, but we also have to have air for the fire. Gary . . . give me your matches."

Lyle crawled to the narrow passageway as Gary dug into his coat pocket and pulled out a small box of wooden matches. He handed it to Shane.

When Shane struck a match, it was like I could *feel* the warmth. We'd been in our igloo for most of the day, and, although we weren't cold, seeing a tiny flame made me really want to be somewhere else. Somewhere *warm.*

It took a few minutes to get the fire started, because most of the branches that we found were as big around as a baseball bat. It would have been better if we had found some smaller branches, but there were none. Dylan volunteered his comic book, and he crumpled up pages to use as tinder. The paper caught quickly, and, after a few moments, the wood began to burn.

Soon, the fire was blazing. Flames licked and curled, and we were bathed in a flickering amber glow. Ten minutes later, it felt like the temperature inside our igloo had gone up twenty degrees! I couldn't believe it. I got so warm that I took my hat and gloves off.

We moved Terry as close to the fire as we could, being careful to make sure that he wasn't so close that his clothing would catch fire. He hadn't said much . . . and after nearly half an hour, he was still shivering. Gary tried to talk to him, but Terry was so cold that he couldn't answer.

Shane and Lyle were whispering to each other, and I couldn't hear what they were saying. But they kept nodding at Terry. Holly and Dylan kept the fire fed. Soon, we'd have to go out for more wood.

Then Shane spoke.

"Guys, Terry isn't getting warmer," he said. He sounded grim. "He has to go to the hospital, and he has to get there soon. We have to get him out of here."

"But Shane," Holly said, "it's still a blizzard out there. We can't see twenty feet in front of us."

"It's going to get dark soon," Shane said. "Then, we won't be able to see a thing. I hate to say it . . . but we've got to leave. If we don't, Terry is only going to get worse."

We looked at Terry. His eyes were closed, his face was pale and gray, and his teeth were chattering. Shane was right: if we didn't get him to a hospital soon . . . .

"Let's go," Shane repeated. "Let's bundle up Terry as best we can and put him on Holly's toboggan. We can pull him out of here."

"What if we get lost?" I asked.

Shane shook his head. "We don't have a choice, Parker," he replied. "The storm isn't letting up. We have to get out of here now . . . for Terry's sake, and for ours."

It didn't take us very long to prepare. The hardest part was getting Terry out of the igloo. He couldn't move well, and we had to do most of the work. I don't even think he could understand what was going on. That's how cold he was.

"Okay," Shane said. He pointed. "We're going to head that way. We know that the town is in that direction, somewhere. We might miss the snowmobile trail, but if we can keep going in a straight line, we should wind up someplace on the main road. Gary and Larry . . . you guys help pull the sled."

We elected Shane Mitchell president of the Adventure Club for a couple of good reasons. He's smart, and he's quick. He comes up with cool ideas.

And usually, he knows the right thing to do in almost any situation.

Were we doing the right thing now?

Whether we were or not, we were about to find out. We huddled together in a tight group and set out through the horrific blizzard.

The snow came up to our waists, and it was like walking in clay. Every step took great effort, and I knew that we would all tire out quickly.

It was getting dark, and fast. Dylan still had his flashlight, and he gave it to Shane, who was in the front of our group. Shane clicked it on, but it didn't provide enough light to see anything. Oh, it was bright, all right . . . but it was snowing so hard that the flashlight beam looked like a short laser.

If there was any good thing at all, it was the fact that we had Holly's sled. Even with Terry's weight on it, the sled slipped smoothly over the newly-fallen snow, and

Shane, Gary, and Larry were able to pull it easily. If we hadn't had the sled, we wouldn't have had any way to move Terry.

Ten minutes went by, and my toes were getting cold. Normally, my boots do a pretty good job of keeping my feet warm. But now my feet were so cold that my toes were going numb. The same thing was happening to my fingers. Ice formed on my eyebrows, and my cheeks and ears felt like they were burning. If we didn't get out of the storm soon, we were all going to be frostbitten.

"We've got to be close," Shane shouted over the wind. "We can't be far from the main road!"

"I . . . I . . . h . . . hope . . . s-s-so," Holly stammered. "I . . . I'm . . . f-f-f-freezing."

"Me . . . t-t-t-t-to," I spluttered.

"Lyle?" Shane called out. "You doing okay?"

"Y-y-y-y-yeah," Lyle stuttered.

"Tony?"

"Oh, j-j-j-just l-l-l-lovely," Tony said. "I think I'll t-t-t-take my coat off and s-s-s-stay a w-w-w-while."

I laughed out loud, and so did Holly. Here we were, in a blizzard with our lives at stake, and Tony still was able to joke about it.

"Dylan?" Shane said.

Dylan didn't say anything.

"Dylan?" Shane called out again from the front of our group. "You okay?"

Still, Dylan didn't say anything.

I turned around. "Dyl—"

My words were cut short. A few minutes ago, Dylan had been right behind me.

Now, he was gone.

7

"Hey, guys!" I shouted through the driving snow. *"Stop! Dylan's gone!"*

Everybody stopped and turned.

"Dylan!" I shouted. *"Dylan! Where are you?!?!"*

There was no answer. But, then again, the wind was howling so fiercely that I might not have heard him. Maybe he didn't hear me.

"He can't be far!" I hollered to the group. "Hang on!"

I backtracked through the snow, calling out to Dylan.

"Dylan! Can you hear me?"

Where did he go? I wondered. I couldn't imagine him

leaving the group, and I didn't see any tracks going away from ours.

My biggest fear was that he got too cold, and just couldn't go any farther. I imagined him face-down in the snow, frozen, unable to move. The thought scared me.

However, in typical Dylan Bunker fashion, he appeared a moment later, trudging toward me.

"What happened?" I shouted over the howling wind.

"My boot came off in the snow!" he shouted back. "I had to dig down to get it!"

"You could have told us!" I scolded. "We were worried about you!"

"Sorry!" was all he said, and we headed back to the others.

"I found him!" I shouted, as soon as I spotted the waiting group.

"What happened?" Shane shouted.

"He lost a boot," I replied. "But he found it."

"Jeez, Dylan!" Tony said. "Next time, tell us! I'd be happy to give you the boot!"

I shook my head and laughed. So did Holly.

We continued on. Still, the blizzard showed no signs of letting up. If anything, it seemed to be getting worse. The wind and snow needled my face and made my skin tingle and burn. My toes and fingers were now completely numb. If we didn't get somewhere warm soon, we would all be in more trouble than we already were.

And then Shane shouted the words that I will never forget:

"The road! We made it to the road!"

My heart flew! I looked up, and, sure enough, we had made it to the main highway that runs through Great Bear Heart. There were no cars in sight, of course, and the road was completely snow covered. In fact, it didn't really look like a road at all, since there were no tire tracks. Just a river of white snow.

But there was no doubt about it. From here, we knew we couldn't be far from town.

We emerged from the woods, running clumsily in the deep snow. While there was a lot of snow on the road, it was a lot easier than trudging through the forest. Shane, Gary, and Terry were jogging, pulling Terry behind on the toboggan.

"Look!" Tony suddenly shouted. *"Rollers!* Right there!"

Although we weren't very far from the restaurant, we could hardly see it in the blowing snow. Even the lighted sign was barely visible.

And there were several trucks out front. As we got

closer, we could see lights on inside.

"We made it!" Holly shouted.

I recognized my dad's truck, and Lyle's dad's truck, too. We bounded right past the vehicles. Shane reached the front door and threw it open.

"Help!" he shouted to anyone who was inside. "We need help!"

Suddenly, there was a flurry of activity. People swarmed all around, pulling us inside, out of the storm. A few grownups went outside, picked Terry up off the sled, and carried him in. Someone threw a blanket over my shoulders. Everyone was talking at the same time, asking questions.

"Terry is really, really cold!" Gary said. "I think he needs to go to the hospital!"

I saw Mr. Martin helping Terry to a chair, but when he realized how bad off his son was, he stopped.

"Help me get Terry to the truck!" he barked. Larry opened the door, and Mr. Martin and Gary helped Terry outside. They got into the truck and headed out slowly. There was a lot of snow in the road, but with his four-wheel drive, I was sure he would make it to the hospital without getting stuck.

And then my dad was standing in front of me, with his hands on my shoulders.

"What happened?" he asked. "Where have you guys been?"

I explained all about the igloo, how we had stayed in it most of the day, and how the blizzard got so bad so fast that we decided to stay there until the storm passed.

"But the Martins showed up," I said. "They were lost, and Terry was really cold. We built a fire, but it wasn't enough to warm him up. So we decided to try and make it back so he could go to the hospital."

Dad told me that all of our parents, himself included, had been worried sick. They all knew we were in the woods somewhere, and they were in the middle of organizing a search party at *Rollers* when we walked in the door. Then he used his phone to call Mom to let her know that we were all okay.

I looked around. Everybody's parents were there. A server brought out hot chocolate for us kids, and coffee for adults. She said they were making a couple of pizzas for us, and they'd be ready soon.

Thankfully, despite all of the trouble we caused, none of us got into much trouble. Dad gave me a lecture about cold weather, but that was about it. Mom was mad because I hadn't told her exactly where I was going to be, but she was more relieved than anything.

And Terry Martin recovered. Frostbite is always

serious, but he made it to the hospital in time. He even wrote a letter. He made six copies and sent one to each of us, saying how thankful he was that we helped him out. I think it was the first nice thing he's ever said to anyone in our club.

Winter finally came to an end. We had a couple of light snow flurries in April, but that was about it. By May, the daytime temperatures were getting warmer, tiny leaves were budding on trees and shrubs, and the flowers in Mom's garden were beginning to sprout. Birds were building nests, darting about with small sticks and grass in their beaks. A heavy rainstorm knocked a few trees over around town. One of them crashed through the roof of the Martin home, causing Gary's bedroom to flood. There were pictures of the damage in the newspaper. Gary, who had his own room, would have to share a room with his brothers until the repairs were finished.

The only problem for us in the Adventure Club is that things were kind of boring. It was still too cold to work on our submarine and get it ready for summer. We were able to have our meetings in our clubhouse, which was cool. And we went mountain biking in the woods, which was a lot of fun. The trails were muddy and wet, and when we were done, we were covered with dirt.

But, for the most part, not a lot was going on. We all

looked forward to summer . . . but waiting for it to arrive was driving us crazy. There just wasn't anything to do. Nothing exciting was happening.

Until one day, in the middle of May, when something happened that will be remembered by everyone in the town of Great Bear Heart. For two weeks, the town was terrorized by a creature we never knew existed.

A hideous beast . . . known as the dog-man.

NIGHT OF THE DOG MAN

AUTHOR'S NOTE

In northern lower Michigan, the legend of the dog man goes back a number of years. My friend Steve Cook of WTCM radio in Traverse City recorded a 'song' about the creature, and the first time I heard it I was mesmerized. It's quite eerie, and describes the legend in great detail. My story, 'Night of the Dog Man', was inspired by this legend, and by Steve's very creepy song. My story, however, is completely fictitious, while the legend of the dog man is believed by many to be a known fact. Whether the legend is true or not is anybody's guess. My advice, however, is to be on the lookout . . . especially if you find yourself in the deep, dark woods of northern lower Michigan.

"And somewhere, in the north woods darkness, a creature walks upright;
And the best advice you may ever get—
Is don't go out at night . . . ."

—from 'The Legend, '97' by Steve Cook (aka Bob Farley)

1

I think what scared everyone the most about what happened that particular May was this:

Myth became reality. A fable became real.

There is an old legend in northern Michigan about a creature known as the dog-man. Supposedly, the beast haunts the woods near Traverse City, which is about seventy miles from Great Bear Heart. The stories about the dog-man are so creepy that lots of people in the whole state get freaked out. A radio deejay in Traverse City even recorded a story about it, and they play it on the radio during the month of October, when everyone is getting ready for Halloween. If you ever hear it, I guarantee it will send shivers down your spine.

On Thursday afternoon we were meeting in our clubhouse, waiting, of course, for the arrival of Dylan. Holly had brought some of her homework, and she was sitting on a milk crate in the corner, quietly working away. Dollar the cat was at her ankles, arching his back and rubbing up against her leg. He found an old acorn and began playing with it. Now that it was spring, Dollar spent a lot more time with us.

Tony Gritter was shooting a rubber band at a spider on the wall, but he was missing with every shot. Lyle and Shane were quietly talking about the work that needed to be done in the submarine. I was reading a book about a ghost ship.

Usually when Dylan arrives, he scurries up the rope ladder and pops his head up through the trap door. We rarely hear him coming.

This time, however, we heard him coming from a long way off.

"Guys!" he shouted. His voice echoed through the forest. *"You gotta see this! You gotta see this!"*

Tony poked his head out the window. Leaves were starting to form on the tree branches, and, within a couple of weeks, the foliage would be so thick that we wouldn't be able to see very far.

Now, however, we had a clear view of Dylan as he ran through the woods. His red hair was being tossed about, and he was carrying something.

"What's he got?" Shane asked, joining Tony at the window.

"Beats me," Tony said with a shrug. "It looks like a newspaper or a magazine."

"Wait until you see!" Dylan exclaimed as he ran. He stumbled and we thought he was going to fall, but he recovered and kept running. Finally, he reached the rope ladder that was dangling from our fort. We could hear him grunting and gasping as he pulled himself up.

At the very moment that Dylan's head popped up through the door in the floor, Dollar batted the acorn he had been playing with. It bounced twice, then hit Dylan square in the forehead.

"Ouch!" Dylan said. "Who did that?!?!"

"Relax," Tony replied. "It was Dollar. It was an accident."

Dylan pulled himself through the floor, then sat on a milk crate.

"Wait until you see this!" he said, waving the latest copy of *The Great Bear Heart Times* in the air. It's a small, local paper that comes out once a week.

"See *what?"* Holly asked, putting her notebook on the

floor. Dollar had climbed into her lap, and she was gently stroking the cat's neck.

"It's true!" Dylan said, unfolding the newspaper to show the front page. "It's really, really true!"

"What's true?" I asked.

Dylan held up the newspaper. On the front was a black and white picture of Lucy Marbles standing next to a tree. There were deep scratches—what appeared to be claw marks—on the tree trunk, about eye-level with Mrs. Marbles. Beneath it was a caption that read:

IS THIS THE WORK OF THE DOG-MAN?

"That's cool!" Shane said. He took a step toward Dylan for a closer look.

"Where was the picture taken?" Tony asked.

"In Mrs. Marbles' back yard!" Dylan replied. "She found the claw marks yesterday!"

Lucy Marbles is known far and wide for one thing, and one thing only: gossip. She's always poking her nose in everybody else's business, spreading rumors about people. Some people say she's harmless, but I don't think it's very nice of her to tell stories about people in town. Especially when the stories aren't even true.

"What's the article say?" Lyle asked. He, too, moved

closer, intrigued by the picture on the front page of the newspaper.

"Mrs. Marbles said that around dark, she heard a loud growl outside," Dylan explained. "When she went to see what it was, she saw a movement in her back yard. She thought it was a dog, but then it stood up on its hind legs and walked into the woods behind her house! When she woke up the next morning, she found these claw marks on the tree!"

"Wow," Holly breathed. She had stood up, and was hovering over the newspaper resting on Dylan's lap.

"Maybe it was a bear," Lyle said.

Dylan shook his head. "Mrs. Marbles said that she's seen lots of bears, and this didn't look anything like it. And besides . . . bears don't walk on their hind legs, unless they're threatened. I read about that in a book."

"It doesn't mean that what she saw was the dog-man," Shane said. "That's only a legend. And besides . . . the dog-man has never been sighted around here."

"Maybe there's two of them," I said.

Holly shook her head. "I doubt it," she said. "I don't think there's even *one* of them. I think it's just a story somebody made up."

"But how do you explain the claw marks on the

tree?" Dylan asked. "And the thing Mrs. Marbles saw?"

"Everybody knows that Mrs. Marbles makes things up," Lyle said. "Besides . . . she said it was near dark, and she couldn't see it very well. Maybe it *was* a bear, and she only *imagined* that it stood up and walked away."

We continued staring at the picture. I had to admit: the claw marks made me a bit uneasy. To think that there was some half-dog, half-man creature lurking in the forest was a scary thought.

"The police came out," Dylan continued. "Officer Hulburt said that he can't explain what kind of animal made the scratches, and even *he* said that he didn't think it was a bear."

Officer Hulburt is a great guy. He and my dad went to school together, and they are good friends. Everyone in Great Bear Heart really likes him a lot.

"Well, that still doesn't mean that there is such a thing as a dog-man," Shane said. "I think, in a few days, everyone in town will have forgotten about the picture, and that'll be the end of it."

Shane was wrong. It was only the beginning.

2

We talked a little more about the dog-man, but then we went on to other things. Summer would be here soon, and we tossed around different ideas and adventures to have. We would, of course, take our submarine into Puckett Lake again. But there were other things that we wanted to do, too. We again talked about a camping expedition in Michigan's Upper Peninsula. We dreamed about hiking through the forest, camping, fishing, and exploring the vast wilderness that makes up a lot of the Upper Peninsula, which is connected to the lower peninsula by the Mackinac Bridge. For sure, a camping trip like that would be great, but we all knew our parents wouldn't ever allow us to do it.

"Are we going to enter the fishing derby this year?" Lyle asked. "I'll bet we could win first prize!"

"Yeah, that would be a lot of fun," I said.

"We'll put it on the list," Shane said. "It's going to be a great summer."

"I hope so," Holly said. "Things sure have been boring these past few weeks."

One thing I noticed, however, was that every few minutes, each one of us would glance at the newspaper on the floor next to Dylan. I stared at it for a moment, and my mind drifted somewhere else, to a place where the dog-man might really exist. I looked at the picture of the claw marks on the tree and wondered: *just what could possibly have made deep scratches like that?* Certainly no animal I knew of. And it was unlikely that the marks had been made by a bear. I knew it was silly, but I felt a little frightened when I looked out the window, down at the thick forest. I imagined a hideous creature, half-dog, half-man, stalking the dark woods around Great Bear Heart.

And yes, the thought did give me the chills.

We wrapped up the meeting after Holly gave us the treasurer's report. She said we had just over three hundred dollars in our club savings account at the bank. We would have had a lot more, of course, but we had to pay Mr. Mullbringer three hundred fifty dollars for destroying his shanty with our ice boat. It still hurt just to think about it. Thankfully, we had been able to earn some more money with our snow shoveling business before winter ended.

"Hey, I've got an idea," Tony said, as we stood beneath the giant maple tree. Lyle was the last one to climb down from our clubhouse, and he pulled the remote from his back pocket, aimed it up, and pressed a button. The rope began to retract and rise into the fort high in the tree.

"What's that?" Shane asked Tony.

"Why don't we go and see that tree ourselves?" Tony replied. "We could take the trail through the woods and come out near Mrs. Marbles' back yard."

"Yeah!" Lyle said. "That would be cool!"

Holly didn't look like she was thrilled with the idea, but she didn't say anything.

"Yeah, let's do it!" I said. "Those claw marks would be cool to see up close!"

"Are you sure we won't get into trouble?" Dylan asked warily.

"We won't be doing anything wrong," Shane replied, shaking his head. "Besides . . . the property that we have to hike through is public land. And I doubt if Lucy

Marbles would care if we went to see the tree in her yard. Come on."

Shane led the way, and we chatted and joked while we walked. There were lots of trails that wound through the woods in and around Great Bear Heart. We knew them really well from our time spent hiking and biking in the summer. Holly, with Dollar following at her feet, walked with her notebook open, reading. She had some sort of test at school in a few days and was going to study every chance she got. Holly studied a lot . . . and her grades showed it. She's been a straight-A student since first grade.

I had been walking, glancing off to the side, when I smacked into Tony. He had been walking ahead of me, and I hadn't seen him stop.

"Hey," I said, taking a step back. "What's up with that?"

Tony didn't say anything. He was staring into the woods.

Ahead of us, Shane, Lyle, and Holly stopped and turned around. Dylan was behind me, and he, too, stopped on the trail.

"What's the matter?" Shane asked.

Tony's eyes were wide. He pointed. *"Look,"* he whispered.

I peered into the forest, around limbs and tree trunks. There weren't many leaves on the trees just yet, but I could see hundreds of tiny green buds sprouting on branches.

But I also saw something else.

A large oak tree, about thirty feet from where we stood. Its tangled limbs spread up and out, crooked and bent, reaching for the sky like bony spider legs. The trunk was big: as big around as a fifty-gallon drum. It's bark was gray and wrinkled, like old leather.

And on the tree trunk, about six feet off the ground—

Claw marks.

3

Holly gasped.

"Whoa," Lyle whispered. Shivers swept through the six of us like an icy breeze.

"Hey," Dylan said, "that's not the tree in the newspaper. We aren't even close to Mrs. Marbles' house."

"It's been here, too," Shane said. "Whatever 'it' is."

"It's the dog-man," Dylan said, very matter-of-factly. "I *know* it is."

We glanced around. Although the day was sunny, the forest now seemed dark and spooky. I shuddered to think that there might be a *real* dog-man wandering around, after all. I wondered if, while we were looking around, perhaps the creature itself was somewhere nearby, watching us.

Waiting.

"Let's get a closer look," Shane said.

"Not me," Dylan said quickly. He shook his head so hard I thought it was going to wobble off. "I'm not going near it."

"Me neither," Holly said.

Shane looked at us. He's a pretty brave guy, but I don't think he was too sure of himself at that very moment.

"All right," he said, "but we've got to tell someone about this. The police will want to know."

"Let's call Officer Hulburt," I said. "He'll know what to do."

We didn't go to Mrs. Marbles' house. Instead, we backtracked through the forest until we reached Great Bear Heart Mail Route Road. Then we followed it into town to the market. Holly picked up Dollar and carried him when we reached the main road.

When we got to the market, we rushed inside and told Mr. Bloomer about what we'd discovered in the woods.

His eyes grew. "I saw a picture of the claw marks in the paper," he said, "and I was wondering about it. But

I thought it was probably a bear."

"It might be," Shane said, "but we thought we'd better call the police and let them know we found another tree with the same claw marks."

"Good idea," Mr. Bloomer said. "You guys can use my phone."

Lyle picked up the phone and dialed the police department. After a minute or so, he was connected to Office Hulburt. Lyle explained everything . . . how we had been hiking through the woods and found the deep claw marks in the tree, just like the ones on the tree in Mrs. Marbles' back yard.

Lyle hung up when he was finished.

"What did he say?" I asked.

"He wants us to wait here," Lyle replied. "He wants us to take him out to the tree so he can see it himself."

Now things were getting exciting! Officer Hulburt was really interested, so we knew that whatever was going on, things were getting serious.

Soon, we saw his police car coming down the highway. He slowed and pulled into the market parking lot, rolling down his window as the cruiser came to a stop.

"Hop in," he said.

Dylan, Holly, Tony, and I got in the back. Shane and

Lyle rode up front.

"This is great!" Tony said. "A ride in a cop car!"

"Yeah!" Dylan said. "And we're not even arrested!"

"Show me where to go," Officer Hulburt said.

Shane pointed. "Just head up the Mail Route Road to the power lines," he said. "We can hike to the trail from there."

Ten minutes later, we arrived at the tree. We felt a little safer with Officer Hulburt, so we followed him as he stepped off the path and waded through the tall brush. We stopped when we were only a few feet away from the tree with the claw marks.

Officer Hulburt peered curiously at the enormous trunk, nodding. "Yep," he said, leaning closer. "Those marks look just like the ones on that tree over at Mrs. Marbles' house. Fresh, too. It looks like these marks were made last night."

I looked at Holly, and she looked at me. I could see the fear growing in her eyes, and I'm sure she could sense the same in mine.

"All right," Officer Hulburt said. "Let's head back. I think we're going to have to investigate this a bit more. I'm not sure what's making these marks, but we're all going to have to be on the lookout."

When I got home that afternoon, I told my mom

what we'd found, and how Officer Hulburt came out to see for himself. When Dad came home from work, he said that he'd heard about it on the radio. He said that Norm Beeblemeyer, the reporter for the *Great Bear Heart Times,* had hiked back into the woods to take a picture of the tree for the next issue of the newspaper.

Everyone was taking the whole dog-man thing seriously. My parents told me to be careful if I ventured out into the woods. Shane, Holly, Dylan, Tony, and Lyle were in the same boat: their parents warned them to be on the lookout if they went into the forest . . . at least until more was known about the mysterious claw marks on the trees.

A week went by, and there were no more reports of trees with claw marks. Nothing out of the ordinary happened . . . until Friday afternoon.

That's when someone else spotted the dog-man. Not only did he spot him, but he took a picture.

And that was just the beginning of what would be a wild weekend in the tiny town of Great Bear Heart.

4

That Friday afternoon, we met at the market—minus Tony. He said he had to help his dad with their boat, and he'd catch up with us in a while. We each bought a candy bar, then walked across the street to Puckett Park, which is right behind the library. The park is right on Puckett Lake. In the summer months, the park is really popular. Huge oak and maple trees stand guard, and their thick foliage offers shade during the steamy months of June, July, and August. Soon, lots of people would be flocking to the beach to picnic and swim.

We sat at a picnic table. There was a man by the beach, throwing an orange dog toy in the water. Nearby, a yellow Labrador retriever waited impatiently for every toss. As soon as the man threw, the dog rocketed into the lake, swimming furiously to retrieve the bobbing object. Holly had left Dollar at her house, which was a good thing. The last thing we needed was a dog chasing our cat around the park.

"Just think!" Lyle said excitedly. "In another couple of weeks, we'll be able to work on our sub! Then we can take it out in the lake!"

Last year, we'd taken our submarine out to look for old slot machines that were rumored to be dumped in the lake. Lo and behold, it wasn't a rumor . . . because we actually found a slot machine and brought it to the surface. It was one of the coolest adventures we'd ever had.

Shane nodded. "Yeah," he said. "As soon as the water warms up, we can get working on her. It'll take a few days to get her ready, since she's been sitting in the boathouse all winter long."

Holly was about to say something when she was interrupted by the squealing of car tires on the highway behind us. Someone had hit the brakes, hard.

We turned to see a red car pull into the library parking lot. The driver wasted no time stopping and rolling his window down.

It was a man, probably older than my dad. He held a camera in one hand.

"I'm not from around here," he said. "You kids know where I can get film developed fast?"

We shook our heads. "Not around here," I said. "Closest place is Indian River or Cheboygan."

"I think I got it!" the man exclaimed.

"Got what?" Shane asked.

"A picture of the dog-man!" he replied. "He was right back there, where the road starts to turn! I saw him cross the highway and go into the woods!"

Our jaws fell.

"Really?!?!" Lyle said.

"Yeah!" the man replied. "I saw him walk across the road on his hind legs. When I turned my car around, he dropped to all fours, then went into the woods!"

"What did he look like?" Dylan asked.

"Scariest thing I've ever seen in my life," the man said. "Dark brown hair all over his body. Pointy ears, like a dog. Long nose, sharp teeth. I tell ya . . . if my wife was with me, she would have fainted!"

"And you think you got a picture?!?!" Shane asked.

"Yeah, I think so," he said. "Just before he disappeared into the woods. That's why I want to get this film developed fast!"

He rolled up the window, backed his car around, and headed south to Indian River.

"Wow!" Lyle said. "I really would like to see that picture!"

"The legend of the dog-man is true!" Dylan exclaimed. "It really, really is!"

Shane spotted Tony on the other side of the road, placed two fingers in his mouth, and whistled. Tony nodded and waved, checked for cars, then darted across the highway. His arms had grease stains on them, and there was a smudge of oil on his cheek.

"Sorry I'm late," he said, taking a seat at the picnic table. "My dad's rebuilding the motor on our boat and he—"

"Never mind," Shane said, and he told Tony about the man that had seen the dog-man, and the picture he'd taken.

Tony was mad. "Aw, man!" he snarled. "I miss all the good stuff!"

"There really wasn't anything to see," Holly said. "But it sure would be cool to see that picture!"

"Officer Hulburt needs to know about this," Dylan said. "The dog-man is probably dangerous!"

"Did the guy say where he saw the thing?" Tony asked.

"Not really," Lyle said, pointing south. "He said it was back there a ways, near the bend in the road."

We were silent for a moment, until Tony spoke. He had a grin that was growing wider by the second.

"Are you guys thinking what I'm thinking?" he asked.

Dylan raised his hands, showing his palms. He shook his head. "Huh-uh, no way, no how," he said. "You guys can go look, but I'm not going anywhere."

"Oh, don't be such a chicken," Tony said.

"Really, Tony," Holly said. "Do you *really* think it's a good idea?"

Tony shrugged. "Maybe, maybe not. I say we buy a disposable camera over at the market, and see if we can get our own picture. Maybe we'll even find his tracks."

As scary as it seemed, it also sounded *exciting.* Things had been so boring for so long . . . but now, we were having fun. Now, things were *happening.*

"We'll vote on it," Shane said. "All in favor of going to see where the dog-man was, raise your hand."

At first, Tony was the only one who raised his hand. Then Shane did, followed by Lyle. Holly shook her head, but she raised her hand. I raised mine.

Dylan just sat there, his arms crossed, shaking his head.

"Oh, come on, Dylan," Tony said. He grabbed

Dylan's hand and raised it in the air, as if he were helping him cast a favorable vote. "We won't even leave the shoulder of the road. What could possibly happen?"

Dylan gave in. "Okay," he peeped, "but I don't think it's a good idea."

And that was that. Someone now had proof that the dog-man really existed . . . and we were going to try to get a glimpse of the creature.

5

We each chipped in a dollar and bought a disposable camera at the market. Then, we headed through town, past the hardware store and *The Kona* restaurant, walking along the sidewalk until it ended. Then we followed the shoulder of the highway past *Rollers* and *Lazy Shores Resort,* a group of small cabins that are rented to tourists during the summer months. As best we could tell, the man was probably talking about the bend in the highway where Farm Road heads west. There were no houses around . . . just lots of trees.

"Okay," Shane said. "Keep your eyes peeled."

Lyle was carrying the camera, ready for action. If the

dog-man appeared, he wanted to make sure he got a picture.

"Look for tracks," Shane said, pointing down. "The thing might have made tracks near the shoulder of the road."

Well, we didn't find any tracks. After searching carefully for a few minutes, we didn't see any sign of the dog-man, either. Like Shane had said: the creature was probably long gone by now.

"Bummer," I said. But truthfully, I was glad that we didn't see the dog-man.

"I'm not bummed," Dylan said. "I don't want to see that thing. I'd have nightmares for years."

"Hang on a sec," Holly said. She stopped and pointed into the forest. "What's that?"

Shane saw what Holly was pointing at, and he, too, shot his arm out, pointing. "It's another clawed tree!" he exclaimed. "I can see it from here!"

Once we knew where to look, we could clearly see the tree . . . and the claw marks six feet from the ground. The tree was a quaking aspen, and the trunk wasn't as big as the oak tree we'd spotted the previous weekend . . . but the claw marks looked identical.

"That guy was right!" Lyle exclaimed. "The dog-man was here, all right! Look at what he did to that tree!"

We stared in silence. Wind rustled the trees, and a car went by on the highway.

"I'll take a picture of the tree, and then we'll head back into town," Lyle said.

"Good idea," Shane agreed. "Then we'll call Officer Hulburt from the market, and let him know that we found another tree with claw marks on it."

Lyle raised the camera to his face, placing the viewfinder to his right eye.

"It's too far away," he said. "I'll have to get closer."

He stepped off the shoulder of the road.

"Be careful," Holly said.

"I will," Lyle replied. "I just want to get a few feet closer, so the claw marks will show up in the picture."

Lyle walked through thick brush and tall grass, closer to the tree line, while the rest of us waited on the shoulder of the road.

"Man, something really freaky is going on," Tony said. "I can't believe this whole 'dog-man' thing is for real."

Lyle had the camera to his eye, bobbing a little bit from side to side to get the best possible picture. He took one step forward—and that's when it happened.

There was a sudden crashing in the woods: branches snapping and twigs breaking . . . not more than a few feet from where Lyle was standing. A dark form shot up from its hiding place.

And we all knew, in a millionth of a second. We knew that if the legend of the dog-man was true, if such a horrible beast actually existed, if the stories were real . . . then Lyle Haywood wouldn't stand a chance.

6

Lyle must have jumped a foot in the air. Holly screamed. Dylan let out a screech and started running, swinging his hands over his head, yelling at the top of his lungs. Tony was so surprised and shocked that when he spun to run away, his feet slipped on the gravel and he fell flat on his chest. He didn't waste any time getting up, though.

I had just started to run when Shane brought everybody back to reality.

"Wait a minute! Wait a minute!" he shouted. "It's only a deer! It's just a deer!"

I slowed and looked over my shoulder in time to see a doe bound into the forest. Lyle was already at the shoulder of the road. He had been running through the tall grass and brush, and now he, too, stopped and turned to look back to where he'd been standing.

Shane was laughing by now. In fact, he was laughing so hard that he fell to his knees and nearly toppled over. Dylan was already at Farm Road. He had stopped running and turned around.

Holly started laughing. Pretty soon, we all were. Even Dylan was laughing as he walked back to join us.

"Man, that thing freaked me out!" Lyle said.

"Me, too!" Holly said between gasps of laughter. "I thought you were a goner, Lyle!"

"The deer must've been laying down in the brush, sleeping," Shane said to Lyle. "You scared it."

"Who scared who?" I asked, and everyone laughed even harder.

"At least I got a picture of the tree," Lyle said.

Dylan made it back to the group. "Oh, man!" he gasped. "Oh, man! I thought it was the dog-man! I thought he was going to eat all of us!"

"Nope," Shane said. "It was only the deer-man." Which brought another round of choking laughter.

"Maybe that's what that man saw," Holly said. "Maybe all he saw was a deer, and he thought it was the dog-man."

"Could be," Lyle said. "He won't know until he gets his film developed."

A car went by, slowing as it passed.

"Come on," Shane said. "Let's head back to the market and call Officer Hulburt. He needs to know that we found another tree."

"And we've got to tell him about the guy that took the picture," Dylan said.

We walked the short distance back to town, all the while talking and wondering if the man with the camera had only seen a deer, and not the dog-man, after all.

From the market, we called Officer Hulburt, who, once again, wanted us to take him to where the tree was.

That makes three, I thought. There were three trees around Great Bear Heart that had strange claw marks on them.

And word was getting around. People were getting nervous, like the time we made Bigfoot tracks and tricked everyone into believing that there was a giant creature roaming around in the woods. The town went nuts, and the six of us had a lot of fun. Nobody ever found out that we were the ones who did it, either.

This time, however, was a lot different. Thoughts of the dog-man roaming the woods were on everybody's mind. People wondered about it, and they talked about it all the time. At *The Kona,* a small restaurant in town, it was the topic of conversation every morning. Norm Beeblemeyer wrote an article about the strange scratches on the trees, and included pictures. Lucy Marbles, of course, was up to her old self, telling everyone that she remembered seeing the dog-man ten years ago, and how it had nearly scared her to death. She created a wild story about the dog-man chasing her through the woods, but said she was able to make it to her house and get inside before it got her.

Some people, however, didn't believe the legend of the dog-man, and they didn't think that the claw marks on the trees were anything to be worried about. These people were sure that it was a bear marking its territory, and there was no reason to be concerned.

However, the next morning, all doubts vanished when the man we saw in the park—the one with the red car and the camera—returned to town.

Not with a picture of a deer.

Or a bear.

For the first time ever, someone had taken a picture of the dog-man.

7

Lyle found out about it first.

He was at the market, buying nightcrawlers and getting ready to go fishing. Puckett Lake was beginning to warm up, and the fishing was getting good.

Instead of going fishing, however, he called me.

"Parker!" Lyle shouted into the phone.

"What!?!?" I shouted back.

"He did it! He really did it!"

"Who did what?"

"That guy! The guy that said he took a picture of the dog-man!"

"Yeah?"

"Well, he did! The picture turned out! It's on the wall down here at the market! I've already called Shane and Tony. Tony is going to call Dylan. Call Holly and get down here now! You've got to see this!"

I hung up and called Holly, explaining what Lyle had told me.

"Is he serious?" Holly asked.

"Sounded serious to me," I said. "And you know Lyle . . . he doesn't make things up! Meet me out front of my house in five minutes!"

By the time we arrived at the market, a small crowd had gathered inside. They were huddled in a group, wide-eyed, staring at a picture on the wall.

"There it is," Lyle said, pointing to the picture as Holly and I strode inside. "Right there."

Shane and Tony were already there, and, like the other people standing around, they were staring at the picture tacked to the wall. It had been blown up bigger, so it was easier to see. The picture was a little blurry, but there was no mistaking what it was.

The dog-man.

The creature was on all fours, near the woods. It appeared to be running, but it was hard to tell for sure because its shape was a little fuzzy. But it was easy to see its long, hairy legs; sharp, pointy ears; and the face of a dog-like creature, its mouth open and its fangs bared as it headed for the woods. It was both fascinating and horrifying at the same time. People around us were pointing at it and whispering cautiously, as if their voices alone would somehow disturb the creature in the picture.

Dylan Bunker showed up, and his whole body shook when he saw the picture. His mouth hung open, limp.

Now, *everyone* in town believed. Seeing, as they say, is believing . . . and here was proof that the legendary dog-man existed. Someone had taken an actual photo of the beast.

And people were wary. Everyone began looking over their shoulder, peering into the woods as they drove by or walked through town.

So, when Shane came up with an idea to capture the dog-man, we thought he was completely out of his mind.

We were in our clubhouse. Originally, we were going to hold our meeting in the park, as Dylan and Holly were nervous about going into the woods. But Shane and Tony brought up the fact that no one had ever been hurt by the dog-man, and, like most wild animals, he probably stayed away from humans. And besides . . . once we got into our clubhouse, we'd be safe, as we were certain that the dog-man couldn't climb trees.

Still, we were all a little wary as we walked through

the forest, heading for our clubhouse. None of us said anything. We looked around, peering among the limbs and branches, looking for any signs of the dog-man, wondering if, perhaps, at that very moment, the dog-man was watching us. Holly had decided to leave Dollar at home . . . just to be safe.

We had just climbed up to our clubhouse and taken our seats on the milk crates when Shane spoke.

"I say we catch him," he said.

"Catch who?" I asked.

"Who else?" Shane replied. "The dog-man."

Lyle got up, walked to Shane, and placed the palm of his hand against his forehead. "No fever," he said. "But you're probably insane. You'd better go home and lay down for a while."

Holly giggled.

"Shane," I said, shaking my head. "There's no way! We can't do that!"

"Why not?" he said with a shrug. "I mean, think about it: there's got to be a way we can catch the thing in some sort of trap without hurting him. If we can catch him, we'll be famous."

"I don't want to be famous," Dylan said. "I just want to be alive."

"He might be dangerous, Shane," Holly said. "Didn't

you see the teeth on that thing?"

"All we have to do is come up with some kind of trap," Shane said.

"You're crazy!" Lyle said. "We're not going to do that!"

"You know," Tony said, staring up at the ceiling with an inquisitive look. "We just might be able to do it."

"You guys are *both* crazy!" Lyle said. "That thing is probably vicious!"

"Maybe so," Tony said. "But so are lions and tigers and baboons, and they're in every zoo in the country."

We went around and around with the topic for nearly an hour. I have to admit, Shane and Tony made good points. They talked about making some sort of snare in the woods not far from our clubhouse. The way Shane described it, we would use a tree—not a huge, towering maple—but a tall, sturdy sapling that we would bend over by tying a rope to the top.

"Lyle, you could climb to the top of the tree and tie the rope," Shane said, "then climb back down. It'll take all six of us to pull on the rope and bend the tree over. We'll make a loop at our end of the rope, and make a trigger latch out of wood. When the dog-man catches one of his legs in the rope, it will tighten around it. That will trigger the latch, which will send the tree springing back up, pulling the dog-man with it."

"Two problems," I said. Everybody looked at me. "One: how do we lure the dog-man to our snare? And two: how do we know when we've caught him? I mean . . . we can't just sit in the woods and wait all day and night for him to show up. And we can't leave him hanging around, dangling from a rope in the tree."

Shane was quick with answers. "We bait him. I don't know what he eats, but if he's a dog-man, he'll probably eat table scraps, like most dogs. We can put some food on the trail to lure him in."

Holly spoke. "But Shane . . . like Parker asked: how do we know when we've caught him?"

Shane thought for a moment. Then he looked at Lyle.

"Hey, Lyle . . . don't you have an alarm system for your house?"

Lyle nodded. "And the garage. It's brand new. Dad installed it a couple of weeks ago."

"What did he do with the old system?" Shane prodded.

"Dad put all of the parts in a box," Lyle replied. "It's in our garage."

"So, you're not using the old alarm?" Shane asked.

"No," Lyle said, shaking his head.

"Then we could rig up the alarm system to our snare," Shane said. "When the snare is sprung, the transmitter sends an alarm to the receiver. When the receiver goes off, we'd know that we caught him."

"Sounds pretty complicated," Dylan said.

"Not really," Shane said. "It wouldn't be that difficult to rig up."

"But when we catch him, then what do we do?" Dylan asked.

"We call Officer Hulburt," Shane replied.

"Maybe we should ask him before we try to catch the dog-man," I said.

"He won't care," Shane said. "Besides . . . he'd probably think that we wouldn't stand a chance of catching him."

And so, we took a vote. Shane and Tony, of course, were in favor. I raised my hand, too.

Holly glared at me. "You think this is going to work?" she asked.

I shook my head. "No, I don't," I replied. "And that's why I'm going to vote that we do it. There's no way we're going to catch the dog-man. Not in a zillion years."

Dylan raised his hand. "Parker's right," he said. "I vote we do it. We aren't going to catch him, anyway."

Holly raised her hand, and, finally, so did Lyle. It was

unanimous. After all, it might be kind of fun to build the snare and rig up the alarm. Besides . . . there wasn't anything else to do, and at least the whole 'dog-man' thing had created some excitement.

We had no idea, however, that the real excitement hadn't even started yet.

8

"Now all we do is wait for the alarm to go off," Shane said, wringing his hands.

The six of us were gathered on a trail in the forest, not far from our clubhouse. We'd spent all day Saturday rigging up the snare and getting things ready. We hunted around and found a tree by the trail that would work perfectly. It was a quaking aspen, tall and narrow like a pencil, but flexible and strong. Lyle climbed up near the top until the tree began to sway. Then he tied one end of the rope to the tree and climbed back down. It took all six of us to pull the rope and bring the top of the tree to the ground. Then Shane tied the other end of the rope around another tree, so it wouldn't spring back up. He and Tony fashioned a loop with the rope that would, hopefully, catch the dog-man by the leg. We hooked it to a trigger apparatus that Shane and Lyle made. It was a latch system made out of wood. The rope looped around and through it, and if the rope was pulled ever so slightly, the latch would spring open. The tree would snap straight into place, snaring the dog-man by the leg and yanking him off the ground.

For bait, we used a bunch of table scraps that we'd saved. We placed them on the ground in piles along the trail, near our snare. We were sure that, if the dog-man really *did* exist, he probably would eat stuff like that.

And Lyle's alarm system was cool. He placed a battery-powered motion sensor next to the tree. When the snare was sprung, the transmitter inside the motion sensor would send a radio signal which would be picked up by the receiver that Lyle would keep with him at all times. If the trap was sprung, day or night, Lyle's alarm would go off. He would immediately call Shane, and then Tony. Shane would call me, and I would call Holly. Tony would call Dylan.

"Man, if the phone rings in the middle of the night, my parents are going to be mad," Dylan said.

"Don't worry," I said. "It's not going to work,

anyway."

After dinner, Holly and I went for a bike ride . . . but we stayed close to town. After all, we were still a little freaked out by the sighting of the actual dog-man. And we certainly didn't want to be out after dark.

The evening was warm. The sun was setting, and it looked like a big egg yolk sinking into the trees. As we rode, we talked about the things we planned to do that summer. We still had a few weeks of school left, but, after that, we'd have the rest of June, and all of July and August. It was going to be another great summer, that's for sure.

And we joked about the snare we'd made.

"That thing is never going to work," I said. "I just voted to do it so Shane and Tony wouldn't get mad."

Holly laughed. "Shane has some good ideas," she said, "but trying to capture the dog-man in a snare is probably the silliest thing we've ever done."

We rode to the market, where we bought ice cream cones. After we finished, we rode back up the hill, heading for home.

When we stopped at my driveway, my mom was standing at the front door, holding the phone.

"There you are," she called out. "Shane is on the phone. He says that it's really urgent."

Holly and I looked at each other, our eyes bugging. If Shane was calling, and it was urgent, it could only mean one thing: the alarm had gone off!

"Tell him we're on our way!" I shouted. Holly and I whirled on our bikes and sped away, lickety-split, heading for Shane's house.

"I have a really bad feeling about this," Holly said as we pedaled through the neighborhood. "I'm really afraid that we were wrong, Parker. What if it worked? What if we really caught the dog-man?"

We'd find out soon enough.

9

Holly and I flew like the wind, pedaling through the neighborhood as fast as we could. We made it to Shane's in under a minute. Lyle was already there, and Tony was just arriving as we whipped our bikes up the driveway. Dylan showed up a moment later, also riding his bike.

"The alarm just went off!" Lyle exclaimed. "Just a few minutes ago!"

"Let's go!" Tony said.

"Don't you think we ought to tell someone?" Holly suggested. "You know . . . just in case?"

"Just in case *what?"* Tony replied. "If we caught him, we *caught* him. We'll figure out what to do from there."

We rode our bikes along Great Bear Heart Mail Route Road until we came to the trail that would take us to where we'd set the trap. By the time we arrived at the trail, we were already out of breath from pedaling so hard. We jumped from our bikes and pushed them into the weeds. Then, we set out through the woods, running like cheetahs.

But the thoughts in my head were racing even faster.

Did we really catch the dog-man? What would he look like? Would we be in danger? What would we do next?

I began to think that this whole thing probably wasn't a good idea, after all, and I wished I hadn't voted to make the dog-man snare.

We continued sprinting, single file, along the winding path that coiled through the thick weeds. Branches whipped past, and our feet pounded the earth like native drums.

And then we heard it:

An unearthly, piercing wail that stopped all of us in our tracks. We stopped so quickly that we piled into each other.

"Holy cow!" Lyle exclaimed. "I think we really got him!"

We weren't very far from the snare, and we continued cautiously, eyes wide, peering ahead of us, waiting for our first glimpse of the dog-man.

Suddenly, we heard a distinct, human-like wail, followed by:

"Don't just stand there, you numbskulls! Get me down!"

Shane stopped and raised his arms in frustration. "Oh, for crying out loud!" he said. "It's the Martins!"

It was true. I'd recognize the voice of Larry Martin anywhere.

We walked a little farther, and, sure enough, the snare had worked, just like we'd planned. In the air, about eight feet off the ground, Larry Martin was swinging upside down, his right foot held fast by the rope. The top of the tree bent under his weight.

Gary and Terry Martin were beneath him, looking up with confused expressions. Gary was scratching his head, wondering what to do.

We stopped walking before they saw us.

"We ought to just leave them there," Holly whispered.

"Yeah," Lyle whispered back.

Dylan giggled, and the Martins heard him.

"Well, if it isn't the Great Bear Heart Goofs," Gary sneered.

"What are you guys doing out here?" Shane demanded.

BREGE

"We're looking for the dog-man," Terry replied. "Same thing as you."

"Looks like we caught him," Tony said. "Gee . . . he's uglier than I thought he would be."

That made the rest of us laugh, but it infuriated Larry, who was gently swaying back and forth, upside down, in the air.

"Get me down!" Larry shouted. *"Right now! Get me down!"*

"You know," Lyle said quietly. He scratched his head. "We really didn't plan for this. How *do* we get him down?"

"We could cut the rope," Shane said, "but he'd land on his head."

"Maybe that would knock some sense into him," I said, which brought another round of snickering.

"Lyle . . . climb up the tree," Shane said. "As you get closer to the top, the tree will start bending. When Larry is low enough to the ground, we can untie the rope around his leg."

"Hey!" Larry shouted again. *"I'm still here!"*

Lyle walked to the tree and scrambled up. As he drew closer to the top, the tree began to bend, slowly lowering Larry to the ground. When Shane could reach him, he untied the rope from his leg. Larry fell to the ground, but he used his hands to break his fall and he wasn't hurt.

"You could've killed me!" Larry snapped.

"Highly unlikely," Tony said. "Next time, watch where you're going."

Gary muttered something under his breath. Terry didn't say anything. Actually, Terry had been kind of nice to us, ever since we saved his life during the blizzard the previous winter.

Larry wasn't hurt, except for a bruised ego . . . which he probably needed, anyway. "Let's get out of here," he said, as he brushed himself off. "Come on, guys."

The Martins walked away, heading through the forest, back toward town.

"Well, at least we know the snare works," Shane said. "Let's reset it and head home. It's going to get dark soon, and I don't want to be out here when the sun goes down."

Lyle climbed back up the tree until it began to bend. When the tree was bent over far enough for us to reach the rope, we grabbed it and pulled. Lyle climbed down the tree and helped, and we reset the snare without too much difficulty. Shane checked the bait piles, which, as of yet, hadn't been touched. Then we started back down the trail.

"I wish I would have been there when that thing yanked him up into the air!" Dylan said.

"That was pretty funny," Holly said. "I never thought about the snare catching one of the Martin brothers."

We found our bikes in the brush and rode back to Shane's house, taking our time, talking and laughing. It sure was funny to see Larry Martin hanging from the tree, screaming to be let down. That was something we'd remember for a long time.

When I got home, the sun was sinking beneath the trees. Holly said goodnight and pedaled to her house.

That night, I dreamed of dog-men. Dozens of them, lurking in the woods, watching and waiting. The dreams were scary, and some of them woke me up. Once, I got up and looked out the window, staring at the street, dimly lit in the glow of the street lamps. A few bats flitted beneath the cones of hazy light, chasing insects. I heard crickets seesawing in the shrubs.

But I didn't see a dog-man.

Still, when I went to bed, I couldn't get the creature out of my mind. I was sure that there were a few others in Great Bear Heart awake at that very moment, doing the same thing I was: wondering about the strange creature that had clawed several trees. In my mind, I could see the hideous beast that the man had photographed near the road, with long, hairy legs, pointy ears, and sharp teeth.

The dog-man.

It took a long time, but I finally sank back to sleep.

And again, I dreamed of the dog-man.

10

Sunday morning was cloudy, bleak, and cold. The sky was gray and seamless, like an enormous blanket. It was a day to stay indoors and read a book, or play a game.

It would also be the day that I would never, ever forget.

I watched television for a while, but there was nothing on. Then I read a book. Dad was out in the garage, working on the car, and Mom was reading the newspaper.

The phone rang, startling me. I was on the couch, and I put my book down.

Did the alarm go off? I wondered. *Is that Shane, telling me to call Holly, telling me that we've caught the dog-man?*

Nope. It was Holly, and she wanted to know if I wanted to go for a bike ride to the park.

"Sure," I said. "I'll be ready in ten minutes."

I slipped a sweatshirt on, made two slices of toast, and wolfed them down before heading outside. I had just pulled my bike out of the garage when Holly rode up. Her hair was in a ponytail that dangled under her bike helmet. She, too, was wearing a sweatshirt.

"It sure is chilly today," she said, as she slowed her bike to a stop.

We rode down the hill, turned the corner, and headed toward the market. There were a few cars parked at the gas pumps, fueling. George Bloomer was outside, sweeping. He waved when he saw us, and we waved back. Then we rode across the street to the park, which was empty. Water lapped lazily at the shore, and the surface of the lake was iron-gray, reflecting the cloud layer above.

"Kind of a boring day, huh?" I said, leaning forward on my handlebars.

"Yeah," Holly agreed. "Not much going on."

We were interrupted by the frantic shouts of Dylan Bunker. He was on his bicycle, pedaling toward us like a madman.

"Holly! Parker!" he shouted. "Tony wants us! Emergency meeting at the clubhouse in half an hour!" His bike skidded to a stop in the parking lot.

"What?" I asked. "Why?"

Dylan shook his head, and it dislodged his bike helmet so it was twisted, covering one of his eyes. He looked funny, until he raised his hand and adjusted the helmet.

"He didn't say," Dylan said. "He just said that it was important. We're meeting at Shane's in half an hour. Tony said he'll meet us at the clubhouse."

Dylan turned around and headed back through town.

"Tony probably got high score on some video game and wants to brag," I said.

Holly giggled. "Yeah, you're probably right," she said.

Shane, Lyle, Holly, Dylan, and I met at Shane's a half hour later, right on time.

"What's the big deal?" Lyle asked.

Shane shrugged. "Tony didn't say. But he said it was important, and he would meet us at the clubhouse."

We rode along Great Bear Heart Mail Route Road. When we came to the trail that led to our clubhouse, we ditched our bikes in the bushes and set out on foot.

"Tony!" Shane called out as we approached the huge

tree where our clubhouse was built. "You up there?"

"He can't be," Lyle said. "I have the remote control, so he couldn't have lowered the rope ladder."

"I guess we got here before he did," Holly said.

But as we approached the tree, we heard a noise on the other side of the mammoth trunk.

We heard a low, deep snarl . . . and we froze.

Another snarl. Louder this time.

A tidal wave of terror washed over us . . . and suddenly, our worst fears came true.

From the other side of the tree trunk, a hideous, dark figure emerged, covered with hair. It was on all fours, and it had pointy ears and a terrible, wolf-like face.

Suddenly, it rose up on its hind legs, and it was as tall as we were.

We were face-to-face . . . with the dog-man.

11

I have never been so close to fainting in my entire life. The terror that I felt when the dog-man emerged and rose up on his hind legs was unlike any other fear I'd ever experienced. Nothing could have prepared me for the awful beast that came out from behind the tree trunk.

Holly screamed. So did Dylan.

The dog-man suddenly lunged for us, front claws raised. Then, one of his paws reached up, grabbed an ear . . . and yanked. The mask came away, revealing none other than Tony Gritter . . . with a grin as wide as the northern sky.

"You!" Lyle squealed. *"What in the world is going on?!?!"*

"This is what's going on!" Tony said. His voice was choked with laughter. "I'm the dog-man!"

"You're . . . *you're* the dog-man?!?!" Shane gasped.

Tony nodded, and he tossed the mask to Shane. "Look familiar?" Tony asked.

"It's your werewolf mask!" Holly said.

"This is the suit that came with it," Tony said, glancing down at his hairy body.

"But Tony," I said, "you didn't wear that mask last Halloween."

"Right, Parker," he replied. "Remember how warm it was in October?" We all nodded. Last October had been much warmer than normal in Great Bear Heart.

"And remember," Tony continued, "that I decided not to wear the mask because it was too hot?"

"Yeah," Dylan said. "I remember."

"Well, I figured nobody would know what the mask looked like, so I could wear it without anyone figuring out that it was me."

"But why did you do it, Tony?" Holly asked.

"Because we were bored," Tony replied shrugging. "Nothing goes on around here this time of year. I got thinking about the legend of the dog-man, and then I remembered my werewolf costume. I thought that everyone in town—including us—could use a little excitement."

Tony went on to say that he was the one who created the claw marks on the trees.

"Look," he said, and he walked around to the other side of the tree, knelt down, and picked up two objects. One was an empty mayonnaise jar, the other a small garden tool that had five pointed claws. "I found this at the thrift store," Tony explained, waving the tool. "I sharpened the points with a file so I could use it to make the claw marks on the trees. Remember? I was the one who spotted the tree with the claw marks when we were walking through the woods. I knew exactly where to look, because I was the one who did it.

"And the time that I told you guys I was working on the boat engine with my dad? Well, that was true . . . but I finished early and carried my costume to Farm Road and into the woods. I put it on, used the tool to make claw marks on a tree, then stood out by the road and waited for a car to come by. That's when that guy turned around and took the picture."

"But Tony," Holly said, "how did you know that he would have a camera?"

Tony shook his head. "I didn't," he replied. "But he did, and it was great! I took off into the woods and hid until he was gone. Then I got out of my werewolf suit, took it home, and ran down to the park. That's where I found you guys."

It all made sense, now that Tony was explaining everything.

"What's the jar for?" Shane asked.

"Watch," Tony said. He raised the jar to his mouth, nearly covering the top with one hand. Then he made a snarling sound into the jar. His growl changed, sounding much deeper than his normal voice! It didn't even sound human!

"But why did you stop?" I asked. "How come you had us come here today?"

"I realized that, sooner or later, something was going to happen. Larry Martin could have really been injured by our snare. Or some animal—a porcupine, racoon, or a rabbit—could have wandered by and got caught. We never thought about that. I figured I'd just end this whole thing before anyone or anything got hurt."

Well, Tony's intentions were good. He was only playing a prank, and he was quitting before things got really out of hand.

Problem was, it was already too late for that, as we were just about to discover. Things *were* already out of hand . . . and in a *big* way.

12

We had just climbed the rope ladder to our clubhouse. Dylan was the last one up, and then Lyle retracted the rope by remote control.

That's when we heard shouting in the distance. At first, we couldn't hear what was being said. But as the shouts grew closer, we could pick out words.

" . . . this way!"

" . . . saw something, over—"

" . . . got to be here, some—"

Shane spoke. "Tony, did anyone see you this morning?"

Tony shook his head. He had slipped out of his

werewolf costume and carried it up to the clubhouse. "I didn't think so," he said. "I didn't put my costume on until I was in the woods behind our house. I had to walk behind a few houses to avoid the street, but I didn't think anyone saw me."

"Somebody must have," Lyle said, "because it sounds like a search party is coming!"

We could hear branches breaking and brush rustling. Although we couldn't see anyone yet, we were certain that whoever they were, they were headed our way.

"What if they find us?" Dylan asked. "What if they see our clubhouse?"

"I think that there are enough leaves to hide it," Shane said. "Besides . . . they'll be looking on the ground. Hopefully, they won't think to look up."

"If they *do* find us," Holly said, "and they figure out that Tony is the one behind this whole dog-man thing, we're going to be in for it."

"I'll just tell them the truth," Tony said. "You guys didn't know anything about it."

"You can tell them that," I said, "but no one will believe it. Especially if they find us all together, and you with your werewolf costume."

Below us, a man emerged through the trees. Then another, and another. Then a few more appeared. I could see Officer Hulburt, and the tall, skinny frame of Norm Beeblemeyer, the reporter for the *Great Bear Heart Times.* And there were a few men that I didn't recognize.

"Let's spread out," someone said. "We'll cover more ground that way. He's gotta be around here somewhere!"

"Somebody must have seen you, Tony," Shane said quietly.

"What are we going to do?" Dylan said. He wrung his hands together nervously.

Shane shook his head. "We don't do a thing," he said. "We stay here, and we stay out of sight. Maybe they won't see us."

There were about ten men in all, spread out through the forest. Norm Beeblemeyer had his camera ready, and one guy carried a big stick. As they walked, they shouted to one another.

"See anything?"

"Nothing yet!"

"We'll get him!"

"Keep your eye out! He's probably dangerous! Mrs. Marbles said that the creature attacked her this morning!"

We giggled quietly. Tony shook his head from side to side. *"It wasn't me,"* he whispered. *"She's just making that up."*

The search party was right beneath us now, and I figured if they hadn't spotted our clubhouse by now, they probably weren't going to.

Shane stood up and crept to a window. *"They didn't even look up,"* he whispered. *"If we wait a while, we'll be in the clear."*

"Let's head east, back toward Mrs. Marbles' house!" one of the men shouted.

We could hear them talking loudly to one another, but as they moved farther and farther away, we couldn't understand what they were saying. After a few minutes, their voices faded completely.

"I'm glad they didn't see us," Dylan said with relief. "We would have had a lot of explaining to do."

"Even if they *did* see our clubhouse," Shane said, "that doesn't mean that they would have discovered us. There would have been no way for them to get up here, unless they came back with a long ladder."

"See?" Tony said with a casual shrug. "No problem."

"Yes, there *is* a problem," Lyle said. "They're following the trail back to Lucy Marbles' house."

"That's what I mean," Tony replied. "They didn't see us. We can go home."

Lyle shook his head. "You're not getting it. They're heading back to Lucy Marbles' house, which means they're heading right for where we made the—"

A loud, long shriek suddenly pierced the quiet forest,

and Lyle didn't have to finish his sentence. The wailing in the woods told us all we needed to know.

Someone had gotten caught in our snare!

13

We were horrified. We'd forgotten all about the snare, and one of the men searching for the dog-man had been caught in it!

"Oh, man!" Tony bawled. "This is all my fault! I didn't mean for the whole thing to go this far! I was just trying to liven things up a little!"

As we listened, other people began shouting. But one thing was as clear as ever: the voice of the man screaming was none other than Norm Beeblemeyer, the reporter for the *Great Bear Heart Times*!

"Get me down!" he was shouting. *"Get me down, right now!"*

Holly laughed. Dylan giggled. Then, we all had to put our hands over our mouths to keep from laughing out loud. Norm Beeblemeyer obviously wasn't hurt, and none of us were all that sorry that he had been the one to get caught in our snare. Norm Beeblemeyer had caused problems for us in the past, and we hadn't even done anything wrong. That certainly didn't mean that we wanted anything bad to happen to him . . . but by the sound of it, Norm Beeblemeyer was fine . . . he was just dangling by his leg, until the other searchers figured out a way to get him down.

"Man, I wish I could see that!" Lyle said. "Norm Beeblemeyer, swinging upside down from a tree!"

We all had a good laugh. But the fact remained that people in Great Bear Heart still believed that there was a horrible dog-man prowling around. Nobody but us knew that Tony Gritter was behind it all. And we were sure the men in the search party would keep looking until they either found something, or thought that the dog-man had moved on.

"Well, I guess I'll be hiding my werewolf costume in my closet for a while," Tony said. "I don't want anyone to find out that it was me, all along."

Suddenly, Shane was grinning like a Cheshire cat. His smile grew wider with every passing second, until I thought that his cheeks would split. Then he nodded a few times. "Not so fast, Tony," he said. "I don't think we're through with the dog-man."

"But Shane," Dylan said, "people are searching for him. What are they going to do when they find out that the dog-man is Tony in a werewolf costume?"

"Oh, if my plan works out," Shane replied, "no one will ever find out that the dog-man is really Tony. No, the dog-man needs to make one more terrifying appearance. A 'grand finale' of sorts. We've done it before, and I think it's time we do it again."

"What are you talking about, Shane?" Holly asked.

"Guys," Shane said, raising his right hand. "Raise your hand if you want to give the Martin brothers the scariest night of their lives."

Well, how could we *not* vote for that?

14

We wanted to scare the Martin brothers in a way that they wouldn't know it was us. The last thing we wanted to do was to make them mad. Then, they'd want to get even with us. No, we had to convince them that they had seen the actual, real dog-man . . . and not know that it was only Tony Gritter in a werewolf costume.

"Whatever we do," Shane said to Tony, "it'll have to be dark, so the Martins won't get a good look at you."

It was near noon on Sunday, and we were still in our clubhouse. Now that we had planned to do something to scare the Martins, we were excited. We weren't adjourning our meeting until we'd figured out just what we were going to do. The commotion in the forest had died down, so we figured that the men had been able to get Norm Beeblemeyer down from the snare. The searchers had moved on.

"I say Tony waits in their garage," Dylan said. "When the Martins go in, Tony can jump out and scare them!" Dylan illustrated this by leaping forward, hands raised like claws, his face all askew.

Shane shook his head. "We can't do anything in their garage or in their house," he said. "That would get us into trouble. We have to stay outdoors. We can be in their yard, but that's it."

We thought really hard. It would be easy to have Tony just leap out of the bushes and scare the Martins when they walked by, but we wanted something better. Something that would terrify them.

We sat quietly for nearly five minutes, thinking. No one said a word until Shane finally took a deep breath and spoke. "Come on, guys," he said. "This can't be that difficult. We have to be able to think of *something.*"

"Wait a minute! Wait a minute!" Tony exclaimed. "That's perfect!"

"What?!?!" Shane replied excitedly. "What's perfect?!?!"

"All three brothers are in the same room!" Tony said.

"Remember? A tree fell on their roof, and Gary's room flooded! They still haven't got it fixed yet. I can go to their window at night and scratch on the glass! Can you imagine how freaked out they'll be?!?! I mean . . . all three of them, in the same room, scared out of their minds? They'll be bouncing off the walls like weasels in a shoe box!"

"That'll be funny!" I said.

"But how will we know when they're in bed?" Holly asked.

"Well, we won't, for sure," Tony said. "I'll just have to wait until they turn the bedroom light off. Then, I'll creep up along the house and scratch on the window. At least one of them will look out, and maybe turn a light on. When they do—"

"They'll see the dog-man looking in!" Lyle exclaimed. "Tony! That's perfect!"

Dylan raised his hand. "But what are *we* going to do?" he asked.

"Nothing," Tony said, shaking his head. "That's what's so great! There's nothing to it! It'll be easy! Nobody has to do a single thing but me. And all I have to do is scratch on the glass, raise my paws, and stare back at them. Then, I'll split into the bushes. They'll never know it's me!"

"Yeah!" Holly said. "And we can hide on the other side of the street and watch!"

I had to admit, it sounded fun. And easy. Tony would simply wait for the Martin brothers to go to bed, then he'd go to work. We would be on the other street, skulking in the shadows, watching.

Sometimes, however, things don't work out the way we plan them . . . and this would be one of those times.

In fact, not only would it not work out as planned . . . but the whole thing was going to backfire.

15

It was Wednesday night, and the sun had just gone down. There was a pinkish-red band of light in the western sky, and stars began to twinkle. It was a typical, late-May night in Great Bear Heart. We had all been able to convince our parents to let us stay out a little later . . . as long as we promised not to go into the woods. True, it was a school night . . . but it was spring and the sun set early.

We were at the market, eating ice cream outside beneath the awning, discussing our plan. Tony carried a large paper sack that held his werewolf costume and mask.

"We'll walk along the sidewalk, toward the Martin's

house," Shane was saying. "Tony, before we get there, cut into the shadows somewhere. Find a dark place where you can put your werewolf suit on. We'll keep walking, and then turn around at the end of the block. If no one is watching, we'll duck out of sight on the other side of the Martin's house. Just keep an eye out for us, and make sure we're hiding before you go up to the Martin's window."

"Sounds like a plan," Tony said, and the six of us headed out, following the Mail Route Road up past the church, heading toward the Martin's house.

When we were getting close, Tony stopped. He let out a low, wolf-like howl. "The dog-man is ready," he said quietly. Then he sprinted off into the shadows.

We continued walking until we reached the end of the block. Then we turned around and backtracked, carefully eyeing the Martin home.

"Everybody ready?" Shane whispered.

"Yeah," Holly said.

"You bet," I chimed in.

"Let's go," said Lyle.

"I'm ready!" Dylan giggled.

"Come on," Shane ordered. "And nobody say a word. Keep an eye out for other people, too."

Here, on this side of town, there weren't very many

streetlights, so it would be easy for us to hide. Which also meant that it would be easier for Tony to escape unnoticed.

Across the street, we could see the Martin brothers' bedroom window glowing. The drape was closed, so we couldn't see inside, but we knew that it was the brothers' window from the pictures in the newspaper.

"Follow me," Shane hissed, slipping into the shadows. He found a lush, full, cedar tree, and we ducked behind it. From here, we had a good view of the Martin's house, but we were hidden well in the shadow of the cedar. Dylan knelt in the dewy grass, and I crept down on my haunches. The five of us were huddled together, shrouded in darkness. All we had to do was wait for the show to begin.

We waited and waited. My legs got cramped.

"Geez," Dylan whined. "How late do these guys stay up?"

"I don't know," Lyle said, "but if they don't go to bed soon, I'm going to have to go. It's getting late."

No sooner had Lyle spoken those words, than the bedroom light in the Martin house clicked off.

"All right!" I whispered excitedly. *"This is going to be good!"*

We waited and watched. Our eyes were now

accustomed to the dark, and we could make out the silhouettes of shrubs and trees on the other side of the street.

A shadow moved. It walked upright, and, although it was dark, we could still see the outline of Tony in his werewolf costume as he crept along the side of the Martin's house.

"Okay guys, get ready," Shane hissed. *"The dog-man cometh!"*

16

The dog-man walked.

Slowly.

Quietly.

The beast-like shadow creeping along the Martin home looked eerie. Even though I *knew* that it was just Tony in a costume, I still got shivers as I watched his dark shape stop directly in front of the unlit bedroom window.

Tony the dog-man raised his right paw . . . and reached for the glass.

Scrit . . . scrit-scrit-scrit . . . screeeeee . . . .

The bedroom window lit up. It glowed amber, dull,

and diffused behind the curtain.

"Wait until they see the dog-man!" Lyle whispered. *"They're going to be scared out of their minds!"*

Across the street, the curtain fluttered. Tony scratched the window again.

Screeeee . . . scrit-scrit . . . screee—

Suddenly, the curtain opened. Plain as day, we could see—

Mrs. Martin, staring out the window!

"Holy smokes!" Dylan hissed. *"It's Mrs. Martin!"*

What was worse: we could hear her terrifying screams. Her shrieks were muffled, of course, because the window was closed, but they were still shrill and loud. Her hands flew to her cheeks and her mouth was agape, and she was screeching like a banshee.

Tony was completely freaked out. Even from where we were, we could see that he, too, was shocked to see Mrs. Martin staring back at him. In fact, he was probably just as shocked to see her as she was to see him. After a moment, he leapt to the right and quickly bounded into the shadows.

"Let's get out of here!" Shane said.

We turned and darted behind the tree, not knowing exactly where we were headed, but certain of one thing: we needed to move . . . and *fast.*

"What about Tony?!?!" I hissed, as we sprinted across a lawn, heading for deeper shadows.

"We'll just have to hope he gets away!" Shane whispered back. *"He'll be all right . . .but if we're spotted around here, somebody's going to figure out what's going on! Then the spaghetti is* really *going to hit the fan!"*

"Too late!" Lyle exclaimed. *"I think it already has!"*

We ducked behind a house and ran through another yard. Thankfully, there were no streetlights nearby and we were concealed in darkness, weaving around hedges and leaping over shadowy bushes.

After we had traveled a few blocks, we whisked into a small clump of forest that split two streets. There, we could melt into the shadows and hide. Hopefully, we'd see Tony soon. He'd have to walk right by us to get home.

"Okay," Shane said between gasps of breath. "That *was* pretty funny!"

"Yeah," I said, "but I thought that bedroom was the one that Gary, Larry, and Terry were sharing."

"Maybe it is," Lyle said. "Maybe their mom was saying goodnight to them at the exact moment Tony scratched on the window."

That seemed like the most obvious explanation.

Holly spoke. "So, now what?" she asked.

"We wait for the police sirens," Shane said. "Mrs. Martin is bound to call the police."

Wow. I didn't like what was happening. This whole thing had started with Tony's prank. We wanted to have fun, but we didn't want to get into trouble.

We waited. The sirens never came . . . but neither did Tony.

"I'm worried," Holly said. "What if Tony got caught?"

"Tony's too smart for that," Shane replied. "He can take care of himself."

"Well, I hope he shows up soon," I said. "I've got to head home in a few minutes, or my mom and dad are going to start wondering where I am."

"Same here," Lyle said.

We didn't have to wait much longer. Soon, we heard the *snick-snick-snickering* of sneakers on pavement. On the next block over, a shadow darted along the sidewalk.

"Tony!" Shane hissed. *"Over here!"*

The figure slowed and turned toward us.

"Tony?!?!" Lyle asked quietly. *"Is that you?"*

"No, it's the dog-man!" Tony replied, as he skirted off the sidewalk and into the small clump of trees where we were hiding.

I breathed a huge sigh of relief. For a few minutes, I

had thought something terrible had happened to him.

"You sure freaked out Mrs. Martin!" Dylan exclaimed, after Tony had found his way through the trees. He was out of breath.

"I didn't mean to," Tony said, shaking his head. "I thought that was Gary, Larry, and Terry's room."

Then we noticed something.

Tony wasn't wearing his werewolf costume.

"What happened to your costume?" Holly asked.

"Don't worry," Tony snickered. "I figured out a way to get rid of it so that no one will ever know we were behind this whole dog-man thing. Let's go. I'll tell you about it as we walk home."

17

Tony Gritter is pretty smart . . . but I have to admit, his quick-thinking that night had been *brilliant.*

"When I saw Mrs. Martin staring back at me in her nightgown," he explained, "I knew I'd messed up. I didn't want to run out into the yard, because if they turned on the porch light, I'd be a dead duck.

"So, I ran around to the back of their house. There was a light on in another bedroom window, and I could hear the Martin brothers shouting and talking. I figured they were in the room. I took off my werewolf costume. When I didn't hear voices in the room anymore, I opened up the screen and dropped my costume inside."

"You *what?!?!*" Shane exclaimed. He stopped on the sidewalk beneath a streetlight, and the rest of us did the same.

Tony flashed a wide grin. "Mrs. Martin got the daylights scared out of her by the dog-man.
Gary, Larry, and Terry were in another room. They got up to find out what was going on. When they did, I opened up their bedroom window and dropped the costume inside. When Mr. and Mrs. Martin find the werewolf costume inside their sons' bedroom, they are going to think that one of the boys is responsible—not only for scaring their mom, but for all of the other dog-man sightings around town!"

"Tony!" Lyle exclaimed. "Great thinking!"

"But the Martin brothers don't know anything about it," Dylan said. "How will they get blamed?"

"Think about it, Dylan," Tony replied. "Mrs. Martin sees a dog-man at the window. There's all kinds of confusion. Then, a werewolf costume appears in the room where the brothers are sleeping. It didn't just magically appear there. Mr. and Mrs. Martin are going to think it was Gary, Larry, or Terry playing a joke."

"And no matter how much the brothers deny it, their parents won't believe them!" I said.

"You bet," Tony said. "And no one will ever know

that we were behind the whole thing. They'll think it was the Martin brothers all along!"

I went to bed that night, wondering. I wondered if Tony's idea had been a good one, and I wondered what would have happened if he'd gotten caught. Then, we *all* would have been in trouble.

But I also felt a warm smugness. If there was anyone in Great Bear Heart who deserved to get into trouble for something they didn't do, it was the Martin brothers. After all, they were always getting away with things and blaming them on others. Not just once in a while, either—but all the time. If they got blamed for being behind the dog-man sightings, it served them right.

And besides . . . nobody got hurt. There was just a little more excitement than usual in Great Bear Heart . . . and there certainly wasn't anything wrong with that.

The following weekend at our clubhouse, we were still talking about what had happened. We hadn't heard anything about the night Tony scared Mrs. Martin, so we were pretty sure that Tony's idea had worked, and Gary, Terry, or Larry had been blamed for the prank. There had been a picture on the front page of the *Great Bear Heart Times* of Norm Beeblemeyer, hanging upside down, swinging from the rope . . . which was really funny. The accompanying article said that there was no further evidence or sightings of the dog-man, but the reporter urged local residents to be on the lookout.

Earlier in the week, Shane and Tony hiked back to our snare and dismantled it. After all, the alarm system still worked, and we might need it in the future.

And the mysterious dog-man was never seen again, of course. We don't know what happened to Tony's werewolf costume, or how much trouble the Martin brothers got into. We thought for sure they would confront us and accuse us of 'planting' the costume in their bedroom. But they never did. They never figured out we were involved.

Spring gave way to summer, and school let out for the year. We did all kinds of things: went fishing, rode our bikes, and sailed our submarine in Puckett Lake. I could write a book about all of the things we did that summer.

By far, however, the funniest thing that happened that year was in August, at the annual Great Bear Heart Chicken Barbeque. I still laugh when I think about it, and, to this day, the six of us look back and know that it would always be the funniest day of our lives.

CURSE OF THE BARKING SPIDER

1

Tony Gritter has always been the club prankster. He was always the one playing jokes and pranks, and coming up with ideas to fool with people, including those of us in the club.

However, Dylan Bunker also enjoyed a good prank . . . but one day, one of his gags didn't go as planned.

Oh, for sure, what happened was completely accidental . . . which is probably why the whole thing was so funny.

Once in a while, Dylan ordered goofy things from the back of his comic books. He would often show us the things he bought—chewing gum that turned your mouth black, an electric hand buzzer that gave a person a shock when you shook hands, a pencil that squirted water—things like that. He got me with the electric hand buzzer. I must admit, it sure surprised me.

Speaking of shocks: one Saturday, when we were scheduled to hold our meeting, Dylan was the first to arrive at our clubhouse. Which was odd, because we almost always had to wait for him to show up before we started our meeting.

But this day, he was excited to show us something. He wouldn't show us right away, but waited until everyone was there before he reached into a small paper bag and pulled out a dark brown bottle with a gray label. It looked like a bottle of root beer, only not quite as big.

"What is it?" Holly asked.

"Read it," Dylan said, handing the bottle to her.

Holly took the bottle from Dylan and held it up, carefully inspecting the label.

"Dr. Tootmore's Magical Barking Spider Powder," she read aloud. *"Guaranteed to Raise a Stink."*

"Isn't that cool?" Dylan said. "Guess what happens when you eat it?!?!"

Holly rolled her eyes and handed the bottle back to Dylan. "That's gross," she said.

MAGICAL
BARKING
SPIDER
POWDER
BREGE

"Yeah," I said. "Who's going to eat that stuff if it makes them—"

"You mix it in with food!" Dylan exclaimed, clearly pleased with himself. "It's a powder. People won't know when they eat it. But soon, they'll be cursed by the barking spider, just like it says on the label!"

"Oh, brother," Shane said, shaking his head and rolling his eyes. "You'd better not try that on *me.*"

"Me neither," Tony said.

"Yeah," Lyle agreed. Holly and I nodded. "We don't want any part of that," I said.

"Oh, come on!" Dylan pleaded. "It'll be fun! I'm going to try it on my mom and dad tonight at dinner!"

"Oh, they're going to love you for *that,*" Holly said sarcastically.

"They'll never know," Dylan said. "I'm just going to make sure I get done eating before they do. I sure don't want to be in the same room!"

We shook our heads. I mean . . . it seemed like it would be kind of funny . . . but it wasn't anything that the club wanted to be involved in.

Dylan put the bottle back in the bag, and we talked about other things. Lyle brought a color brochure about a place in Michigan's Upper Peninsula where kids went camping for weeks at a time. There were a lot of cool pictures, and we spent nearly an hour going over the brochure, dreaming about camping in the forest, sleeping beneath the stars, and foraging for our own food. It would be really cool to do something like that.

We didn't get much accomplished at the meeting, other than the usual stuff. It was time for Dollar to get his shots from the veterinarian, so we voted to allow Holly to use money from our club savings account at the bank. No matter how little money was involved, when it came to club finances, we always took a vote. It just seemed more official that way.

We adjourned our meeting after voting on going to the Great Bear Heart Annual Chicken Barbecue the next day. The Great Bear Heart Athletic Club hosts it every year, and the food is always really good. After eating, we would head into the woods for a long mountain bike ride, following the old railroad bed that wound around Puckett Lake and into the town of Indian River a few miles away. It's a fun trail, and we always see a lot of cool things. Once, we saw a huge bald eagle swoop down to the lake and snatch a fish. That was awesome.

Holly and I walked home together. The day was hot, and there wasn't a cloud in the sky. Dad wanted me to mow the lawn, but after that, I was going to the beach to swim. Holly was going to come, too, along with Lyle.

"I can't believe Dylan bought that powder," Holly said, shaking her head and grinning.

"If he puts it in his parents' food, I don't want to be anywhere near there," I said. "His whole house is going to smell."

After I mowed the lawn, I went to the beach. Holly and Lyle showed up, and we played frisbee in the water. There were a lot of people around, too, because the day was so nice. Sunday was supposed to be even warmer, which would be great. It would be a great day for a bicycle ride.

As it turned out, however, we wouldn't be going on a bike ride. In fact, Sunday wouldn't go at all like we thought it would . . . and it all began when Dylan Bunker showed up at my house in the morning. I had never seen him in such a mad panic before—and when he explained what had happened, I did two things: first, I gasped, then, I laughed so hard that I cried. I knew right then that the day was about to get really interesting . . . and very, very smelly.

2

"You did *what?!?!*" I exclaimed in disbelief. Dylan had already told me once, and I had heard and understood what had happened . . . I just couldn't *believe* it.

"It wasn't my fault!" Dylan insisted. "It was an accident! My dad is in charge of making chili for the annual Great Bear Heart Chicken Barbeque today. Well, I left my bottle of *Dr. Tootmore's Magical Barking Spider Powder* on the counter at home . . . and my dad took it by mistake, thinking that it was his chili powder! I mean . . . he took the whole jar!"

By this time, I was laughing so hard I could barely speak. My sides hurt. "Where . . . where is . . . is he . . . now?" I choked.

"This isn't funny, Parker!" Dylan said. "Oh, man! My dad has already left to make the chili! He's at the park right now!"

I looked at my watch. It was almost noon.

"The barbeque starts in just a few minutes!" Dylan said. "We've got to get there and stop my dad!"

With that, Dylan sped away on his bike. I ran to the garage, hopped on my own bicycle, and took off after him, shaking my head and laughing as I rode.

I stopped near the market, made sure there were no cars coming on the highway, and crossed over to the park. There were people everywhere, forming a long line, waiting for the food to be served. The annual chicken barbeque draws a lot of people every year.

Near the library, Dylan dropped his bike in the grass and ran toward the picnic tables, bumping into people in an effort to get to the cooking area. Holly, Lyle, Tony, and Shane were seated at a picnic table, waiting for Dylan and me.

I rode my bike up to the table.

"What's up with Dylan?" Tony asked.

"His dad accidentally took his jar of *Dr. Tootmore's Magical Barking Spider Powder*," I replied.

"So what?" Lyle asked.

"So, his dad is in charge of making the chili for the barbeque today. He mistakenly thought that Dylan's bottle was his chili powder."

"Oh, no!" Holly said, covering her smile with her hands.

Shane, Tony, and Lyle laughed.

"He's over there, right now," I said, pointing to the row of barbeque grills. "He wants to stop his dad before he uses the powder in his chili."

We watched as Dylan hustled over to his father. We could see them talking, and then Mr. Bunker got busy with a few of the other cooks. Dylan reached down, picked up his bottle of barking spider powder, and made his way through the crowd of people, heading toward us.

"Boy, you sure got lucky," Shane said, as Dylan approached. "Good thing you got your powder before your dad used it in the chili!"

Dylan's face was white as he sat down. He held the bottle up, unscrewed the lid, and turned it upside down.

The jar was empty.

"I was too late," Dylan said sheepishly. He combed his fingers through his red hair. Holly's eyes grew, and her jaw fell. "He used the whole thing?" she asked.

Dylan nodded.

Somewhere, a bell rang.

"Food's on, everyone!" a man shouted. "Come and get it!"

"What are we going to do?!?!" Dylan asked.

"All we can do is watch," Lyle said.

"Yeah," I agreed. "And hold our noses."

3

The line of people began to move.

We saw smiles, handshakes, flashing paper plates. It was the height of summer, the weather was great, and everyone was happy and bright. Lucy Marbles laughs really loud, and we could hear her cackling as she stood in line. Grills opened up like trunks of cars and barbeque chicken was served, along with corn on the cob and mashed potatoes. Farther down the line stood Mr. Bunker, wearing a white apron . . . and serving heaping bowls of steaming hot chili.

"Man, which way is the wind blowing?" Tony asked warily. "I don't want to be downwind when that powder starts to do its dirty work."

Shane snorted, and I giggled. Even Holly smiled. Sure, the whole situation was kind of gross, but there was something funny about it, too.

Dylan was a nervous wreck. He fidgeted on the picnic table bench, watching suspiciously as people carried their plates and bowls of chili to their tables. Several people walked around with large pitchers of lemonade, filling plastic cups for people.

"What am I going to do?" Dylan whimpered.

"I know what we're *not* going to do," Shane said.

"What's that?" I asked.

"We're *not* going to eat the chili," Shane replied with a laugh.

George Bloomer, owner of the Great Bear Heart Market, was manning one of the grills. He spotted us.

"Hey guys," he called out, waving a pair of tongs. "Food's great! Come and get it!"

"We will," Tony called out.

"Well, what are you afraid of?" Mr. Bloomer asked with another wave of the barbeque tongs.

"Barking spiders," Shane whispered with a chuckle. We laughed.

"You know," Holly said, "if we're going to eat, we'd better do it now, before anything happens."

So, the six of us picked up paper plates and plastic utensils from a nearby table and got in line. The thick aroma of barbeque chicken made my mouth water as people threaded past the row of grills and tables of food. Soon, we were seated at our picnic table, our plates piled with chicken, corn, and potatoes . . . but no chili!

The food was awesome, and I wolfed down my chicken like I hadn't eaten in days. In no time at all, I had barbeque sauce all over my fingers and hands. Then I rolled my ear of corn in a small pad of butter and gnawed on it as Lyle told us about a huge fish that he'd caught earlier in the week.

Mr. Bunker spotted us, and noticed that we didn't have any bowls of chili.

"Hey, you guys," he called out, raising a large stirring spoon. "Chili?"

"No thanks, Mr. Bunker," Shane replied. He rubbed his belly. "We're pretty full."

"Suit yourselves," Mr. Bunker said with a shrug, and he went back to serving bowls of his chili.

When we finished, we dumped our used plates and utensils in the garbage bin, then returned to our picnic table. So far, all was quiet.

"Maybe the stuff doesn't work," Lyle said. He turned to Dylan. "Did you try it on your parents last night?" he asked.

Dylan shook his head. "No," he said. "I tried it on our dog, though."

"What happened?" I asked.

"Man!" Dylan replied. "He was ripping them so bad, I made him leave my room!" He waved his hand in front of his nose. "It was awful!"

"Maybe it just takes a little while before it starts to work," Tony said.

Most of the people had been seated, and many of them had finished their food. They were all chatting and laughing. In Great Bear Heart, almost everyone knows everyone else. There aren't many strangers in a town of only a couple hundred people.

Lucy Marbles cackled and stood up. Suddenly, we heard a sound that we recognized immediately. Mrs. Marbles let out an embarrassed gasp and placed her hand to her mouth. People around her raised their eyebrows. Some of them looked away.

Dr. Tootmore's Magical Barking Spider Powder was starting to work . . . and it was time for the fun to begin.

4

Several people giggled. Lucy Marbles muttered something, then hurriedly walked away. A couple of people turned their heads, and a woman scrunched up her nose and winced.

"Whoa!" Tony said. "That was a loud one!"

"I think I felt the ground shake," Shane laughed.

"Sounds like Mrs. Marbles stepped on a duck," Lyle said. We giggled.

And that was just the beginning.

There was a group of four men standing near a trash can. They were talking among themselves . . . until they suddenly waved their hands in front of their faces. The men's smiles faded into frowns and grimaces.

"Hey, Fred!" one of the men said. "Warn us before you do that again! Hoo-wee!"

"You're gonna kill us all!" another man said, turning away, but still waving his hand in front of his face.

"Silent, but deadly," one of the other men said. "Whew! That one was *bad,* Fred!"

Near the row of barbeque grills, Mrs. Norberg, the Great Bear Heart librarian, accidentally dropped an empty paper cup on the ground. When she bent over to pick it up, you guessed it: we heard a noise like gurgling thunder. She stood up quickly, looking very embarrassed.

All around the park, everyone who ate chili was feeling the effects of *Dr. Tootmore's Magical Barking Spider Powder.* We heard several more offending sounds. People were squeezing their noses and holding their breaths. Several people were hurrying away from the picnic area. Even more were getting into their cars and leaving. Everyone wanted to get away as quickly as possible.

As for us? We were safely away from the line of fire, so we were doing more than just giggling—we were keeled over in laughter. Even Dylan, who had been so worried, was now doubled over, laughing so hard that I thought he was going to choke. Holly was covering her eyes with one hand, but she had a grin so wide that I could see all of her teeth. Tony was on his knees, laughing so hard that he had to hold his stomach with both hands.

A familiar voice suddenly boomed from behind us, and we turned.

"Well, well," Officer Hulburt said. He was carrying a bowl of chili. "Did you kids get enough to eat?"

We straightened up and tried to stop laughing, but we still had guilty grins on our faces.

"Plenty," Shane said.

"Good," Officer Hulburt replied. "Dylan, your dad's chili is awesome. Better than last year, even. Spicier. This is my third bowl."

"You're *third* bowl?!?!" we all exclaimed.

"You ate *three* bowls?" Holly asked.

"Sure did," Officer Hulburt said, scooping a spoonful of chili. "My stomach feels kinda funny, though. I think I'm going to get a glass of lemonade. You kids need anything?"

"A gas mask," Tony whispered, and that caused all of us to burst out laughing. Officer Hulburt, however, hadn't heard Tony's comment. "What's so funny?" he asked.

"Oh, Tony's just being goofy," Shane said.

Officer Hulburt shrugged and began to walk away.

Suddenly, he let loose with an eruption that seemed to make the earth tremble! It stopped Officer Hulburt in his tracks. He turned to us, mortified.

"Whoops," he said. He was blushing. "S'cuse me." Then he quickly hurried off.

"Let's get out of here before we're all poisoned!" Lyle chortled, and we all laughed as we leapt up from the picnic table and ran down to the beach. We stopped near the shore of Puckett Lake, out of breath, but laughing so hard that we nearly passed out.

"I think that one killed all the trees in the park!" Shane said, holding his nose.

"Hope nobody lights a match!" Tony exclaimed, and that brought about another fit of laughter.

Dylan, who had been so freaked out at first, now thought the whole thing was as funny as could be.

"Nobody better tell my dad!" he said. "If he ever finds out about this, I'll be in a ton of trouble!"

Shane raised his hand. "I vote that we keep this our secret, and we vow never to tell anyone."

We all raised our hands, and I spoke up. "Except," I said, "for me. I might write a story about this one day."

"Yeah," Lyle said. "It would make a funny story."

"But you can't let anyone read it until we're older," Dylan warned.

"Promise," I said.

And that was that.

I don't know how long we stood at the shore, cracking jokes and laughing about what had happened. We laughed until our sides hurt.

Soon, Shane announced that he had to leave to help his parents with some errands. It was already the middle of the afternoon, and he said we'd postpone our bike ride until later in the week. Tony, too, had to leave to help his dad with their outboard motor, which had conked out again. Holly, Dylan, and Lyle left the park and went home.

But not me.

I walked over to a picnic table and sat, staring out over the lake, thinking about all of the fun things we'd done over the past year. Our haunted schoolhouse had been a huge success, but, after what had happened, we knew that we wouldn't be doing it again. Not at the schoolhouse, anyway.

Our snow shoveling business had been a success, too, and we'd earned a pile of money. The ice boat that we built was demolished and Dylan Bunker could have been seriously hurt. But he wasn't, and now when I think about him being pulled across the ice, I always smile.

And the blizzard! Wow. That was scary! But, thanks

to some quick thinking, we made it out okay, including Terry Martin, who suffered from frostbite. The whole dog-man thing had started out scary, but when we found out it was only Tony in his werewolf costume, well, then it was funny . . . especially when we'd been able to pin the whole thing on the Martin brothers!

And I still laugh when I think about Dylan Bunker and his bottle of *Dr. Tootmore's Magical Barking Spider Powder.* In my mind, I can still see Lucy Marbles and that silly look on her face, and old Mrs. Norberg when she bent down to pick up the cup.

And Officer Hulburt had eaten *three* bowls of chili! We thought that he might explode!

I sat alone in the afternoon sun, and I started laughing again. I laughed so hard that tears came to my eyes and rolled down my cheeks. Some of the people in the park noticed. They stared at me like I was out of my mind, but I didn't care. A woman saw me laughing and walked to where I was sitting.

"Young man," she said with a scowl, "what in the world is wrong with you?"

Still laughing, I shook my head. "Nothing in the world is wrong with me," I said. "Everything is just *perfect.*"

As she turned to walk away, she accidentally let one

rip . . . and I laughed so hard I almost fell off the picnic table bench! The woman stormed off angrily . . . another victim of *Dr. Tootmore's Magical Barking Spider Powder.*

To this day, there are probably a few people that remember seeing a dark haired kid in the park on a sunny afternoon, sitting alone, laughing like a crazy person.

And that's just fine. I didn't care what anyone thought about me. All I cared about were the important things: having fun, laughing, kidding around. I cared about my family, of course.

And—

I cared about my friends.

Shane, Holly, Tony, Lyle, and Dylan. They were the absolute best friends I could have ever hoped to have.

As I watched the sun dance and sparkle on the shimmering waters of Puckett Lake, I knew one thing was certain:

The Adventure Club would last forever.

Oh, sure, we'd all grow up, probably get married and have houses and families and do all the things that grown-ups do. We probably wouldn't get together like we did when we were in school. Maybe some of us would move away.

But right now, none of that really mattered.

What really mattered was that I had my

memories . . . and man, they were *good* ones. Nobody can take those away. No matter what happened, I knew I would always have my Adventure Club memories to look back on. And I knew that I would always smile when I thought of Shane, Holly, Tony, Lyle, and Dylan.

Don't let anybody tell you different: if you have good friends, you have everything. That's what *really* matters.

THE END